It's always been Us

L.L. Diamond

L.L. Diamond

It's Always Been Us
By L.L. Diamond
Published by L.L. Diamond

Cover and internal design © 2019 L.L. Diamond
Cover design by L.L. Diamond/Diamondback Covers
Cover Art by Flystock and Nate Rosso via Shutterstock

ISBN-13: 978-1-7342783-2-3

Facebook: https://www.facebook.com/LLDiamond
Instagram: @l.l.diamond
Twitter: @LLDiamond2
Blog: http://lldiamondwrites.com/
Austen Variations: http://austenvariations.com/

L.L. Diamond

Other titles from L.L. Diamond include:

To the loyal JAFF fan base.
Thank you for everything!

Chapter 1

The early evening air held a balmy quality that made my skin sticky and my thin linen tank top cling to my body like a second skin. South Carolina summers tended to be uncomfortable, and tonight resembled a typical southern evening—hot, humid, and causing even the best-tempered person to want to sit in a cooler full of ice. I set my hands behind me on the thin blanket and relaxed back in a futile attempt to catch even the smallest tendril of passing breeze while the people around me continued to set up for the Marysville Fourth of July celebration.

"Jena! There you are!"

I opened my eyes as my younger sister, Ellie, and her fiancé, William, approached the picnic blankets I'd set out to reserve our spot. Ellie placed Freya, their almost two-year-old daughter, on the quilt next to me while William scanned the park.

"This is a great spot," said William. He pointed to a basket he'd set on the somewhat dry grass; there hadn't been much rain this summer, and the lack of water had started to turn the grass a dry brown. "We brought wine and antipasto if you're thirsty or hungry."

Ellie laughed and shook her head. "We also have water, fruit, and a cake if you'd prefer. When is Charlie coming?"

"She said she'd be here before the music began." Marysville always had a large Independence Day concert in the park. Every year, a series of local bands performed live while nearly the entire town spread out on the lawn and enjoyed the warm, albeit humid, weather. The night was always topped off with a magnificent fireworks display that lit the entire town.

William pulled Ellie into his lap as Freya giggled and plopped down on her mother's lap.

I startled when my sister grasped my wrist.

"Before I forget to tell you! The florist called before I walked home to change. They've confirmed they can get the lilies and roses I requested for the wedding. I also confirmed with the resort on the island. We can hold the wedding on the beach, and if you remember, they have that amazing open tent for receptions. They're willing to set it up nearby, so we're closer to the water."

William and Ellie planned to marry in a few weeks, hurrying since Ellie recently discovered herself pregnant with their second child. At least Ellie, Charlie, and I were wedding planners. We knew the ins and outs of whom to call to plan a ceremony and reception in a short period of time. Ellie and William desired a small affair, wanting nothing more than their closest friends and family in attendance, which would make things simpler. The day would be lovely, knowing Ellie's romantic sense of style and the local island resort they'd selected as the venue.

"It sounds amazing," I said with a smile. "Are we still going dress shopping tomorrow?"

"Definitely! Hopefully, I won't outgrow whatever I pick out before the wedding."

"If you do, you'll wear one of your everyday dresses and still look amazing," said William, resting his chin on Ellie's shoulder with a grin. "I don't care if you come in a burlap sack. As long as you say 'I do.'"

When the two of them got all mushy like that, I found it difficult to keep my eyes from tearing up. I so wanted what they had! I'd thought I'd found it; however, the man I'd thought was "the one" turned into a dirty rat instead of Prince Charming. Unfortunately, he wasn't the first dud I'd dated, and I feared he wouldn't be the last.

A guitar strum resonated through the thick air, pulling my gaze from William and Ellie to the stage where the first band now prepped for their show. The drummer twirled his drumsticks, and the bassist played a few notes before they both nodded to the singer, who counted them off, and brought the music to a roaring start.

Freya let out a loud yell, and when I glanced at her, she clapped and bounced in her Daddy's lap while everyone around us watched her enthusiasm and laughed.

"There you guys are!" Charlie, the third musketeer in our wedding planning business strode forward with her older brother, Brandon, following close behind. "We've been looking all over for you."

Brandon set down their basket and ice chest before he handed his sister the blanket. She spread it out by Ellie and took a seat while Brandon sat beside me. "It's kind of sticky tonight, isn't it?"

"A little," I said. "It's not so bad as it's been in the past, though."

He winced and shook his head. "No, two years ago was the worst. Poor Ellie sweltered out here."

Ellie had certainly been miserable. She'd also been eight months pregnant with Freya at the time. I glanced at my sister, who was certainly not so uncomfortable this year. "She would've worn a bikini that year if she'd thought she wouldn't be lectured by someone."

He chuckled and leaned back, propped on his hands, as I peered over and traced the edge of his sculptured jaw with my eyes. Ellie and Charlie were my best girlfriends, but Brandon and I had been besties for as long as I could remember. My dad had always called us two peas in a pod.

When we were young, Ellie and I both had a tomboy streak in us, but while Ellie would go make mud pies in her dresses, I adamantly refused to wear any sort of a skirt. How could Brandon and I run through the woods and build forts if, as my mom used to say, "I had to worry about keeping my legs together like a lady?" Brandon also taught me how to spit for distance. Not many girls could claim they could spit four feet, but I could. It was by no means a world record, but I was proud of it. I adamantly refused to fish with him, though. No way was I going to put my hands on a slimy worm or a wriggling fish! Blech!

Brandon and I both changed a great deal as we grew up, but we remained close. He beat up Denny Howard for stealing a kiss from me in seventh grade, he kept creepy Collins Hardy from cornering me behind the bleachers during a home football game, and when I didn't have a date for senior prom, he escorted me. He was the best big brother stand-in a girl could've asked for. We even wrote tons of letters to each other when he joined the Army to help pay for college. I, on the other hand, stayed close to home by attending the University of South Carolina.

Once upon a time, he'd dated, but come to think of it, I hadn't seen him with a woman in ages. I don't know why he stopped. He was a great guy and deserved the best—not that I knew anyone good enough for him.

"Jen?"

I snapped out of my daze, my eyes meeting his. "Huh?"

He smiled and lifted his eyebrows. "You were staring at me."

"Oh, sorry. I zoned out there for a minute."

"A penny for your thoughts?"

I laughed and shook my head. My cheeks warmed. "Nothing earth-shattering."

He nudged his shoulder to mine and gave me a mischievous grin. "Come on. It had to be something."

With a sigh, I leaned over and pushed him a bit with my shoulder this time. "I was only wondering who would be good enough for you."

He turned his head to face me straight on. "Do you mean a woman?"

"Yes, Brandon, I meant a woman. You *were* into those the last time I checked."

He held up one of his fingers. "Number one, I still like women. I adore women actually." Another eager finger popped up to join the first. "Number two, I'm not interested in anyone I've met recently, and . . ." His ring finger joined the first two. "Number three, it would be weird having you set me up, so don't."

My eyes rolled toward the red and purple-tinged sunset above. "You don't have to get a burr up your butt about it."

"I don't have anything up my butt. I know what I want, and I'm waiting patiently for it. End of story." What on Earth did that mean? An odd glint in his eye made me want to ask, but the way he spoke made the air around us thick and oddly awkward. My breath caught in my chest, requiring me to clear my throat.

"I never uttered one word about setting you up," I said, "but point taken. Geez."

He scooted over and opened the cooler. "Here, I brought you some tonic water and that Cupcake vodka you like." He pulled a glass out of the nearby basket, and in no time, held a vodka tonic in front of me. "Maybe this will set your head straight."

"I resent that, Taylor. My head is already screwed on straight." He didn't respond, but instead, popped the top off a beer, taking a long draw. I didn't know which one since I couldn't see the label, but it was no doubt one of the local craft beers he liked so much.

"That, Barrett, is up for debate."

A sharp, shrill inhale filtered through my nostrils, and I punched him in the arm.

"Ow!" he said, chuckling. "I'd forgotten how much that hurts."

As the sun slowly began its descent, one band left the stage and another got fired up while everyone in the park continued to eat, drink, and visit with their neighbors. Grant Davies, William's father, joined us and played with Freya while Ellie and William cuddled to a ballad crooned out by the woman on the stage.

The relaxed atmosphere and the music lulled me into a rather happy place until Charlie's hard voice ground out, "What the fuck is *he* doing here?"

"Charlie!" said Ellie. Fortunately, Grant had walked Freya to the playground where he currently kept her occupied in the toddler swings.

"Freya isn't nearby, and seriously, do you see who it is?" She whispered that part loudly while she jerked her head back toward the trees. I shifted to peek around Charlie, but when I saw the man's face, my stomach plummeted. Charlie's language, no matter how vulgar, was right on the money.

"I thought he moved to Charleston." Brandon spoke right next to my ear.

I cleared my throat and swallowed. In no way was I going to allow my ex-boyfriend Connor Willoughby to ruin my evening! "He did. He found a job with a larger real estate group in the city just before . . ."

I'd first met Connor when the girls and I were looking for a new office space for our company. He'd found the amazing red brick and white trimmed house we'd bought and used for our wedding planning business as well as our home. Connor had asked me to have dinner with him the day we finalized the sale, but with Ellie's unplanned pregnancy, I needed to be there for her instead of for myself. I'd told him no. We'd run into each other from time to time, usually at the grocery store or the gym. Then, at about the same time William came back into Ellie's life, I caved and started dating him. We lasted about six months—

"I didn't realize they were still seeing each other."

My eyes followed Brandon's gaze to Lacey, the woman Connor was sleeping with when he dumped me. He hadn't made that fact a secret when he ended things between us. He'd merely said he found someone else. Asshole.

"Apparently so."

"Tell me the truth." Brandon's honeyed voice dropped lower, and his breath grazed against my ear, tickling me.

"What?"

"Are you still hung up on him?"

I looked back to the stage. I had no desire to have Connor think I sat over here pining for him. He could date the entire skanky part of Charleston for all I cared. "No, but I do still want to put Ex-lax in his daily mochaccino."

"So, I can beat him up?" Brandon sounded downright giddy at the idea.

"No, it's okay. I think more than anything I'm annoyed that he found something with her that's lasted this long while I'm still alone. I just don't want him to think I miss him, or that I'm still in love with him."

Brandon's arm wrapped around my middle and dragged me between his legs, my back to his chest. "I can help with that."

"He knows you're my best friend. I doubt he'll buy it."

Warm, soft lips pressed a kiss to my temple. "But maybe he will."

I spent the rest of the evening using Brandon as my lawn chair and doing my best to forget Connor and his girlfriend had parked their blanket no more than ten yards from us. In all honesty, Brandon worked out pretty well as a makeshift lawn chair. I was comfortable, I had a fresh drink whenever I felt the urge, and I had a pillow on his shoulder when I needed to tilt my head back to see the fireworks.

William, Ellie, Freya, and Grant were long gone by the finale. Like me, William and Ellie lived across the street from the park. So, once they put Freya to sleep, they could watch the fireworks from their patio, leaving no point in remaining out here with a sleeping toddler. Charlie had also made herself scarce by the end of the night. She saw a couple of friends and decided to hang out with them for a while.

I vaguely remembered *1812 Overture* and the bursts of brilliant color exploding in the palette of the clear night sky. The evening had cooled but Brandon brought a quilt that he let me huddle under while he held me from behind. I found myself warm, comfy, and in this contented sort of haze that faded into nothing.

"Come on, Jen. Let's get you home."

"Hmm?"

He chuckled and kissed my cheek. "You're such a lightweight. It's bedtime."

I sighed and snuggled closer to the warmth. "But I'm comfy here." An arm hooked under my legs, and I wrapped my arms around his neck.

"You owe me for this."

Everything went dark until my lovely heat source disappeared. I opened my eyes. I lay on my bed while Brandon stood over me. When had he had the time to get me home? "Where are you going?"

He pulled off my Converse slip-ons and drew the comforter and sheets out from under me. "I'm putting you to bed, and then I'm going home."

I fumbled with the button on my jean shorts and groaned. "Too tight to sleep in. I need these off." When my legs were free, I managed to take off my bra while leaving my top on. As Brandon pulled the covers over me, I grabbed his wrist. "Don't go." I tugged him down toward the mattress. "It's too late. Just stay here with me."

Two clunks echoed around the room as he removed his shoes. A moment later, my favorite source of heat curled up against my back. "Better?" he asked.

"Definitely. Love you. You're the best."

Chapter 2

When I opened my eyes the next morning, the lingering scent of his cologne and an imprint on the pillow were the only hints of Brandon's presence during the night. It was a Saturday morning, but Brandon had worked for his father's veterinary practice since he'd graduated from Clemson's veterinary school. The two of them traded Saturdays, which meant this morning was probably his turn to work, or else I'd still be cuddled up to him. Brandon always slept in on his Saturdays off.

I dragged myself from the covers and looked down at my horribly wrinkled linen tank top. "Lovely," I said hoarsely before clearing my throat. I stared at my bare legs and winced as the image of Brandon removing my shorts flashed in my mind. How was I going to live that down? I'd only had two vodka tonics. I'd been drinking water too. How did I get that bleary from two measly drinks?

My jean shorts lay sprawled on the floor, so I picked them up and threw them into the hamper with my rumpled top on my way to the bathroom. A shower and a toothbrush with plenty of toothpaste did a lot to revive me before I stood in front of my closet. Ellie, Charlie, and I were going shopping for wedding dresses today. I needed to look nice. It wasn't every day you helped plan your sister's wedding.

William and Ellie embodied the perfect couple—not that their relationship had begun in a typical or perfect way, but now, you'd never know they'd ever had problems. Ellie had met William while on a tropical vacation on the other side of the world, the two of them became swept away in a whirlwind romance until Ellie discovered William was married. Of course, nothing was as cut and dried as it appeared to Ellie at first glance. Between his divorce and Ellie's insecurities, it took two years before they managed to reunite and work toward becoming the happy couple I knew. William finally popped the question last month.

I chose cocoa-colored paper bag trousers and my white silk top, fastened a two-tier gold necklace around my neck, and slipped on my nude Jimmy Choo knock-offs. When I looked at the result in the mirror, I tilted my head and smiled. I always found it funny that Charlie, Ellie, and I all had our own unique style that carried over into our work. I tended toward the upscale and cutting-edge, Ellie gravitated toward the romantic, and Charlie, when she wasn't wearing athletic clothing, had this sort of Boho-chic look and excelled at planning ceremonies for those who wished for something more eclectic or even retro. Really and truly, Charlie mostly dealt with the bottom line since she was the numbers girl. We were strikingly different, but it worked for us.

I shook myself out of my own head and walked out of my bedroom to find Charlie in the kitchen. "What are you doing?"

"I'm out of tea. I thought you might have some hiding in one of the cabinets."

I lived on the second floor of the house we used for our offices, the upstairs was renovated as living space, and Charlie lived in the studio apartment on the third floor. When we first moved in, Ellie and I both originally lived on the second floor, though I'd briefly moved into the garage apartment when William and Ellie got back together. Once they found their own house, I moved back in, taking Ellie's old room since it was larger. The income from renting out the garage apartment didn't hurt either.

"Check in the top cabinet on the left of the stove."

"Ah-ha! I knew you'd have some." She set the kettle on the burner and pulled a mug from the hook. After she put the tea bag into her cup, she looked at me, leaning her hip against the counter. "I caught Brandon doing the walk of shame this morning."

I sighed and shook my head. "You know it's not like that. It was late. I didn't want him on the road when he'd been drinking."

"Oh, please!" She laughed and reached for the whistling kettle while I opened the fridge to grab a yogurt. "He had a grand total of two beers the entire evening. He also carried your drunk ass all the way back here when you passed out, and, I'll have you know, he didn't swerve once."

I jerked up, and a sharp pain ripped through my skull. "Ow!" I grabbed my head with one hand while I held on to the refrigerator door with the other. I needed to remember that the freezer was just above me. "How do you know he carried me back?"

"Who do you think hauled the basket and the cooler back here?" She dunked her teabag while she gave me that look, one that wanted answers that didn't exist. But really, now, what did she expect? Brandon and I were friends—we'd always been friends and we'd always be friends. Nothing was going to change that.

"You act as though he's never spent the night with me before. Are you trying to protect his virtue?" I couldn't help but laugh. "Because I can tell you that disappeared a long time ago when he dated—"

"Eww! I don't want to know that!" She grabbed the mug and pointed at me. "Keep your filthy mouth shut! Gah!" An exaggerated shudder wracked her body while she hurried out the balcony door.

"My filthy mouth?" I shouted after her as Charlie's footsteps clomped up the stairs until the door closed on the third floor. That girl possessed a vocabulary that would make a sailor faint.

With Charlie back on her own turf, I ate breakfast in peace until the alarm system beeped and the downstairs door opened and closed.

"Jena! Are you ready?" Ellie called up the stairs

"Yep, text Charlie to meet us out front." I grabbed my purse and my sunglasses.

"Already done."

Marysville boasted a decent bridal boutique on the other side of Main Street, so we walked a few blocks to an old factory on the river that had been renovated and split into quaint shops with rustic exposed wood beams and antique brick walls. The shop might have been small, but it had a great stockroom and could order from just about any designer that produced wedding gowns. We recommended it to clients often.

Ellie pushed the door open as Emma, the owner, bounded around the counter to greet us. "I'm so glad you're here, Ellie!" she said, gushing as she always did. "I ordered a few gowns, based on your measurements, that I thought might fit the description you gave me."

"You didn't have to do that." Ellie's eyes widened as Emma took her hands. "What if you don't sell the extras?"

"They're such beautiful gowns." Emma waved away Ellie's concerns. "And you send so much business my way. I'm sure I'll sell them before too long. While they do fit what you want, they have a classic simplicity that will be appreciated by others. I'm certain of it."

She ushered us over to an alcove of plush chairs and a small old-fashioned sofa. "Let me grab you some champagne." Emma gave a sudden jump. "Oh! I even have sparkling cider for you, Ellie."

After Emma hurried away, I chuckled. "Emma didn't skimp on the coffee this morning."

"I heard that!" called Emma from the back.

Charlie and Ellie burst out laughing while my face burned. "Sorry, Emma!"

She walked back in with two bottles in one hand and three mismatched crystal champagne flutes between the fingers of the other. "Honey, I'm not offended. I love my store. It's an honor for me to help find the perfect dress for some lucky girl's big day. I just adore it!" Emma loved just about everything. Her social media posts always had multiple exclamation points and smiley faces per sentence. I'd never met anyone else with so much boundless enthusiasm and positivity as Emma. "If only I could get my own knight in shining armor to propose, my life would be set."

I sank into one of the overstuffed chairs. "How is Gregory?"

"He's great. He had a piece to write for the paper today. I'm sure he's holed up in that dark study of his, typing away at his laptop." She set the glasses down and poured our drinks.

"Now, let's get started, shall we?" She pulled back the curtain in the back corner of the shop to reveal about ten dresses. "These are the gowns I ordered. Of course, you're welcome to browse around the racks and see if I have any others you'd like to try. Don't be shy. Whatever you want or need, just let me know."

"Why don't I start with what you've ordered?" Ellie stepped up and began shifting through hangers, holding up each dress and appraising it. She turned to Charlie and me and did a little happy dance, jumping slightly up and down with a squeal. "I'll be right back out."

Emma closed the curtain behind Ellie and rubbed her hands together. "I can't wait to see which one she picks." With my sister busy putting on a gown, Emma fluttered around, straightening racks and primping the silk flowers arranged all around the quirky yet elegant room.

It was the tell-tale whoosh of the curtain that drew our attention back to Ellie. She almost tiptoed over to the enormous gilded frame mirror propped against the wall under a crystal chandelier. She rotated back and forth, scrutinizing the dress.

"What do you think?" asked Charlie. "It'll work well if you get a baby bump in the next two weeks."

"Charlie!" I stood and walked over behind Ellie, looking over her shoulder. The gown was simple with tiny straps, an empire waist, and a light layer of sheer silk over pearly satin. "It's beautiful—simple, classic. The line is graceful too. A veil would add a lot to it."

"I agree." Ellie bit her lip and smiled. "I do adore it, but I don't want to settle for the first one. Let me try on the others."

Emma shuffled her back behind the curtain, and after every change, Ellie emerged, each time wearing an exquisite gown. Emma had gone all out searching for the dress that would suit my sister best. After trying on what seemed like twenty, Ellie emerged in the first gown she'd tried. "This is the one. I keep comparing this one to the dresses that followed. It's perfect."

I brought over a veil with a floral comb and tucked it just above her braid. She'd fixed her hair like she hoped to wear it for the ceremony, which would definitely be helpful with selecting a headpiece. Emma brought a large mirror and held it up behind Ellie so she could see the effect for herself.

"I love it. Thank you, Emma."

"Sweetie," Emma said with a drawl. "You still have shoes to pick out."

Charlie gave a guffaw. "She's not wearing shoes, Emma. She's going barefoot." The woman's eyebrows lifted nearly to her hairline, but Ellie waved her hands in front of her before Emma could say a word.

"Since the wedding is on the beach, I don't want to wear a pair of fancy shoes only to have them fill with sand. Instead, I found these pretty pearl and lace barefoot sandals on Etsy."

Emma's face lit with a grin. "Oooh! Those sound interesting. You'll have to bring them by so I can see them. I've never considered something like that for a wedding. Most of the brides I've dressed had a platform or a temporary flooring that covered the sand. They didn't have the ceremony on the beach itself."

Ellie's expression became wistful and she shrugged. "William and I fell in love on the beach, my favorite maternity photo is the one Micah took at sunset with the water behind me, and we'll join our lives on the sand overlooking the ocean. The beach will always be a special place for us."

I scanned the store. "So, we have a dress, we have a veil, and we have shoes—sort of. You'll need a garter, of course, and some jewelry."

"Grant gave me his wife's pearls, and I found this gold strand with a pearl at the end that can hang from the clasp down my back." With a turn, Ellie peered over her shoulder at the back of the gown. "I think it's just low enough for it too."

"You bought that strand a couple of weeks ago," said Charlie. "What would you have done if it hadn't worked?"

"I have a couple of dresses I could wear with it. Plus, William loves it." My sister looked off to the side with this curve to her lips like she had some delicious secret.

"Oh, no! TMI!" I turned her little butt around to face the mirror. "We don't want to hear about anything that would put that kind of smile on your face."

Charlie's head bobbed as she relaxed back in her seat. "I agree! It was bad enough when the two of you still lived in the house and I could hear your headboard knocking against the wall."

"You could not!" Ellie's hands landed on her hips and she whirled around, her cheeks pink. "You would've said something. You couldn't have held it in, and you know it."

Charlie's eyebrows lifted and she gave an incredulous bark. "You think I wanted to tell you that? Besides, soft music was enough to drown out the bump, bump, bump. You couldn't help it that my bedroom was directly over yours."

Ellie put her palms to her cheeks that had turned even a brighter blush than before. "I'm so embarrassed!" She hurried back into the changing room while Emma pulled the curtain closed behind her.

"You didn't have to bring that up," I said, my eyebrows lifted.

"I know I didn't. It just sort of popped out. You know I'm bad about doing that with you two."

"I bet Ellie knows plenty about you and Jensen Worth that she doesn't say in front of people."

"I certainly do!" called Ellie from behind the curtain.

"I don't want to talk about Jensen." Charlie's expression grew hard and her fingers tightened on the armrest. "Can we drop this?"

Ellie stuck a thumbs-up through the part in the fabric. "No problem whatsoever!"

Charlie finished off her glass of champagne and poured another large serving. She always turned sour at the mention of Jensen's name, which was understandable. Charlie and Jensen dated from her freshman year until we graduated high school. Everyone expected them to marry, but unfortunately, that never happened. Ellie, Brandon, and I didn't even know exactly why they broke up after graduation that year. As it was anywhere in the world, however, small towns thrived on gossip, and poor Charlie's break up didn't escape the scrutiny. Nosy old biddies still asked her if she'd heard from Jensen from time to time.

After Emma's, we had lunch planned. We'd have to shake Charlie from her funk, or we'd all suffer for the next few hours.

When Ellie emerged from the dressing room, she passed her dress to Emma along with the veil, and we followed her to where the garters were on display. My sister picked one up and wrapped it around her fingers as if she might shoot it like a rubber band.

"What do you think, Charlie? After William removes this with his teeth, who should he toss it to?" Her eyebrow arched and she stifled a few giggles. "I could throw you my bouquet or maybe throw it to Jena?"

A rough chuckle came from Charlie's lips. "You throw your flowers at me, and I *will* exact revenge." An evil, crooked grin started to spread across her face. "You won't know the time or the place, but I'll get you, my pretty, and your little dog too." The three of us burst out laughing, and with one ridiculous threat, Ellie took care of Charlie's mood.

Ellie shot the garter in Charlie's face before she turned around and took a pretty crocheted piece from the rack. "This one's gorgeous." She handed it to Emma. "I'm fairly certain I have everything I need and I'm starving. Freya woke me up early this morning and I ate nothing but toast to settle my stomach."

Emma added the garter to the rest of my sister's purchases. "Don't worry about a thing, honey. I'll get these bagged up and run them over first thing Monday morning, so you don't have to carry them all over town. Charlie's and Jena's bridesmaid dresses will be back from being altered. I'll have those too."

"That would be amazing. Thank you."

"Of course! You girls have a wonderful time at lunch."

After we exited out to the sidewalk, we walked further down until we reached Riverfront, a restaurant that stood partially on stilts with an amazing deck I would kill for. One of my favorite things to do was sit on the deck first thing in the morning with a pastry and coffee, watching the ducks swim lazily and the dragonflies hover near the surface of the water. This morning, the cooler weather made sitting outside and along the railing preferable to being indoors. The rambling river flowed along the edge of the deck as I relaxed in the sun, closing my eyes and savoring the atmosphere. I opened them when the server placed a mimosa in front of both me and Charlie and a sparkling fruit drink before Ellie.

"I heard Brandon spent the night," said Ellie before taking a sip. She had this innocent air about her, but something in her tone made my spine stiffen.

"He does that from time to time. You know that."

My sister's eyes narrowed as she studied me for a moment. "Okay."

"What does that mean?"

Ellie shook her head and reclined into her seat while Charlie gave a slight snort. "Nothing. Nothing at all."

A part of me wanted to challenge her, but today was for her wedding preparations and a special time. I didn't want to argue with her. "What else do you need to arrange for the big day?" Changing the subject seemed the best solution, but why did I feel like my sister meant more by her statement than I was willing to understand?

Chapter 3

My phone rang, startling me from my email to the caterer for the Landry-Hollister wedding. Smiling at the name and picture emblazoned on my cell phone screen, I picked it up, touched the icon to answer it, and put it to my ear. "I didn't expect to hear from you today."

Brandon's voice vibrated through the earpiece. "We haven't been able to hang out for a week, and that new romcom you've been wanting to see is at the movie theater. I thought you might want to go."

"Ooh! The one with Ryan Reynolds?"

"That's the one." His warm laugh floated through the line. "I know how much you enjoy his sparkling intellect."

A giggle escaped before I could control it. "He has a sparkling something."

"Gross. If I'm going to sit next to you for ninety minutes of a romcom, I don't want to listen to you slurping on your own drool."

"Ha ha."

"Movie starts at seven-fifteen. I'll pick you up at six-thirty. Do you want me to shower? I know how much you love the smell of dog and antiseptic."

"You are so stupid," I said, laughing. "You'd better shower, or I'll go see the movie by myself."

"I have to go. Mrs. Crawford is in exam two. She thinks her dog swallowed her son's school eraser. See you later."

"See you later." With a smile, I ended the call and bit my lip.

"Who was that?"

My head shot up to my sister, who leaned against the door frame. "Brandon. That new Ryan Reynolds movie is at the theater. We're going to see it tonight."

"He makes you happy."

I lifted a shoulder and swiveled in my seat to face her. "Of course, he does. He's my best friend."

Ellie casually stepped inside and closed the door. "The two of you have been best friends for as long as I can remember, but your relationship has changed. The problem is that I don't think you see it."

"I'm not sure what you mean. Nothing has changed. We're just the same as we've always been."

She stood behind the chair in front of my desk. "Have you ever noticed that neither of you dates?"

"I date," I said. My tone was defensive to my ears, but I didn't understand what she was hinting at. "I dated Connor for six months. I loved him. Remember?" I took my mug from the coaster on my desk and swallowed a gulp of tea and winced. It was cold.

My sister folded her arms in front of her. "I don't think you truly loved Connor." I opened my mouth to speak, but her voice came out instead. "I think you're searching for what you already have—you want what you have with Brandon because you don't think you can fall in love with him. Besides, I never liked Connor."

"I know you didn't like him. That much was obvious, but you never told me why."

After a sigh, Ellie relaxed and leaned against the chair in front of my desk. "When I saw you and Connor together, you weren't the Jena I know. You weren't truly yourself—you were this too-perfect version of what you thought Connor wanted. You never relaxed with him the way you do with Brandon. You're nothing more than Jena when you're with Brandon. He brings you out of your reserve like no one else does."

My hand clenched on my desk and I rubbed my thumb back and forth on the joint of my index finger. "I slept with Connor. I had sex with him. How could I not reveal myself?"

"You may have shared your body with him, but did you hold back your heart and soul? Did you lose yourself in his embrace or did you actively think about every move you made? If you held back, you only showed him what's on the surface. Brandon knows everything else—what's in your heart, your hopes and dreams. How much of that did you give Connor?

"Even on the island, William and I spent hours talking. We bared our experiences and the way they shaped us as well as what we wanted from the future."

A part of me wanted to throw out that he hadn't told her he was married, but it would've been a cheap shot. I couldn't be that mean. "Why are you bringing this up now?"

"Because Charlie and I have both noticed that the two of you are in this sort of stalemate. You date men who are all wrong for you while he doesn't date at all. How long will it take you to take a chance on each other?"

"Forever," I quipped. "He's like a brother to me."

"No, he's not." Ellie rolled her eyes and shook her head. "I'd be willing to bet money that Charlie never, ever slept in the same bed or cuddled with her brother the way you do. She'd gross out at the thought too."

"We're friends, Ellie." The tone of my voice dropped. Ellie was wrong. No ifs, ands, or buts about it. We were friends. Nothing more.

"Don't get mad. I don't want to see you alone for years because you didn't recognize what was right in front of you."

"When people are in a stable relationship," I said with some bite. "They sometimes want to see everyone around them settled. Is that what this is?"

Ellie straightened. "No, I love you. I don't want life to pass you by. I believe if you take the chance, you won't regret it."

After the door closed behind her, I stared at my phone. Brandon? Really? I'd never considered him that way, so why would my sister think I was on any level in love with him? I hadn't even seen him since the Fourth of July. We'd spoken on the phone almost daily, but that was normal for us.

The rest of the day, regardless of how hard I tried to purge Ellie's words from my brain, they lingered and popped back up like a bad penny at every opportunity. By the time I left work, I badly needed a glass of wine while I changed and waited for Brandon.

When I finally made it upstairs, I filled a glass of merlot and took it to my room. I swapped out my grey dressy pants for a pair of jeans, leaving on my nice black blouse and topaz jewelry. After I washed my face and put on a light layer of fresh makeup, I ran a quick brush through my hair and swapped out my dress shoes for my black strappy sandals. The clock read six when I was ready, so I took the rest of my wine out to the balcony with a book while I waited.

I read for no more than five minutes when, "You've been waiting for me?" startled me from Lady Sarah's angry tirade against the earl.

As Brandon climbed the last few steps, I shrugged. "No big deal. I've been wanting to finish this book."

"Did you?"

My eyes, which had strayed to his white button-down shirt, popped back up to his face. "Not yet, but I'm close."

He picked up my glass and finished the last sip. "Are you ready?"

"Do I need to change?"

Glancing over my clothing, he shook his head. "No, not at all. You look amazing."

An odd prickling tickled the back of my neck. Did I have a mosquito back there? I rubbed my neck before I picked up my glass and my book. "Let me grab my purse."

"You don't need it and you know it." He took what was in my hands and put them on the table. "Let's go." He entwined his fingers with mine and led me down the stairs. As I followed, my arm brushed the solid muscle of his back, making me swallow hard and shake my head. Why was I thinking about his muscled back?

His charcoal-grey SUV was parked in front of the house. He opened the door for me to get in. Brandon had always been a gentleman—even when we were young. While I fastened my seatbelt, I watched him walk around the front of the car, the natural red highlights in his sandy hair standing out in the evening sun.

"Are you okay?" he asked once he'd climbed behind the steering wheel. "You're acting a bit weird."

I leaned my head back against the headrest, and our eyes met while he started the car. "It's been a long day."

"Tell me about it! I had to remove two of those rectangular erasers we used in first grade from that dog's stomach. Do you know that woman didn't want me to shave much of his hair? 'He has a show in two weeks,'" he mimicked in a high-pitched voice. "'He can't have a bald spot.'" He gave a disgusted snort. "Because it's better that the dog dies of infection, right?"

I grinned and brushed my hair behind my ear. "What did you do?"

"I did what she asked me to do. I didn't let the tech do the shaving in the event she had a fit. Dad found it hysterical, but he's been practicing forever. He dealt with that crazy woman long before I ever got licensed."

"Where are we going?"

His low chuckle filled the front seat of the car. "You sure you're okay? We're going to the movies, remember?"

"Well, yeah. I just meant what theater? There are about three theatres within about twenty minutes."

A wide grin lit his face. "Unless they don't have the movie, we always go to the same place. You know that."

"True." Brandon loved this one cinema that happened to be the closest in Marysville. They had these cushy leather chairs, allowing you to relax while you watched the movie, and they served dinner. They did have awesome cheeseburgers and onion rings. I'd have to jog every morning for the next week to make up for splurging tonight—we always splurged when we ate there.

Since it was a weekday, only six people turned up for the new release. We arrived early enough to get our dinner order in before the previews started, and since lately the advertisements and trailers never took less than thirty minutes, we had our food delivered right before the start of the movie. When I had nothing but crumbs left on my plate, I shifted back to rest against his side while I sipped my wine and watched the film. My attention riveted to the screen when a certain actor emerged from the shower shirtless with a few rivulets of water trickling down his very well-defined pecs.

A hand brushed my chin and I about jumped out of my seat. "What are you doing?" I made sure my wine hadn't splashed over the rim of the glass as I sat straight.

Brandon took a swig of his beer and grinned. "Just checking."

"For what?"

"Drool," he said with a chuckle that made me want to slap him silly.

"We've seen plenty of movies with women you enjoy watching. I don't do that to you."

Someone in front of us turned around to stare for a moment, so I took a gulp of my wine as I relaxed to the other side of my chair.

When the credits finished, I stood, running my hands along my clothes now that the theater had turned on the lights. I didn't think I'd spilled my wine, but I wanted to make sure. My black top would be forgiving, but my jeans might stain.

"You don't have a spot on you."

"No thanks to you," I said with a huff. "How many movies have we watched where you had that ridiculous starry-eyed expression at the woman's *endowments*? Did I interrupt or keep you from enjoying the view? No. I rolled my eyes and watched the movie, hoping you'd picked it for something besides the pair of tits on the screen."

His eyebrows jerked toward his hairline. "Wow, you said 'tits.'"

"You would." I walked off, his footsteps behind me getting closer when I neared the exit. Of course, the only word he'd hear was tits. He may have been my best friend, but he was obviously still of the male persuasion.

He grabbed my hand and nudged my shoulder with his. "Come on, Jen. You know I'm just picking on you. We've always given each other crap, and it's never bothered you before."

I stopped and slumped in my spot. "I know. Chalk it up to a weird day and that you startled me."

"Tell me what happened?"

I dragged a deep breath into my lungs and blew it out. "Just some observation Ellie made. It's ridiculous really—not worth talking about."

"Are you sure?"

"Yes, I'm sure."

Brandon squeezed my hand. His expression resembled what I remembered from when we were kids. "You know what we need?"

"What?" I gave him a side-long glance. When he asked a question like that, almost anything could come out of his mouth.

"Ice cream."

He tugged my arm and crooked his finger in my direction. "Come on. You know you want to."

"I'll be exercising all week to get dinner off, and you want ice cream?"

"You don't need to exercise. You have an incredible body and you know it."

I reluctantly followed bumping his side when I caught up. "Since when have you checked out my body?"

"I'm a guy, Jen. Unless the woman is a member of our family, we look. We can't help it. It's encoded in our Y chromosome."

My burst of laughter made a couple strolling nearby turn and look. "You're insane." He pulled me down to the river path and toward the best place to get ice cream in Marysville.

Whenever I walked inside The Fountain, I always felt transported back in time to when we were young. Brandon, Charlie, Ellie, and I would stop by the shop on our way home from school for milkshakes or a sugar cone with our favorite flavor. In the past ten years, the classic pink, mint green, and white décor never changed—the air even smelled the same, hinting of sugar cones, candy sprinkles, and fresh waffles.

"Well, look at you two!" Mrs. Jennings clasped her palms together, her eyes zeroing in on our joined hands. This wasn't the first time she'd seen us hold hands, but the gossip around town would have us engaged because we happened to be tonight. I'd bet my right kidney on it!

Brandon gave the same lopsided grin he always wore for the ladies. "Hey there, Mrs. J. How've you been?"

"Oh, about the same, but you know, not much knocks me down." Her eyes narrowed as though she were trying to read our thoughts. "So, two sugar cones. Jena will have bubblegum but you, Brandon Taylor, are harder to guess. Your order never stays the same." She scanned the selections under the glass doors in front of her. "Butter pecan?"

"Close," he said with a curve to one side of his lips. "Rocky road."

She tapped her pointing finger in his direction with a flutter of her eyelashes. "That would've been my second guess." Aside from being a major gossip, Mrs. Jennings always flirted with the good-looking men who frequented her shop. With Brandon, it began when he returned to Marysville after four years in the Army and she noticed the boy who'd been replaced by a mature, strapping young man. I just loved that she was one of the few people who could make him blush if she got going.

"How's your daddy?" she asked him, leaning over to scoop my cone first.

"He's good. I'll be sure to tell him you asked."

Mrs. Jennings winked while she handed me my cone. "You do that, sugar." I bit my lip as a faint glimpse of pink appeared on his cheeks. "How about you, hon? Your daddy still seeing that divorcée who just moved into town from Charleston?"

I nearly dropped my ice cream, barely holding on at the last minute. "Ma'am?"

"Oh? Did he not tell you girls?" She gave a tut and started digging into the container of Rocky Road. "He brought a lady in here on the Fourth, they ordered two cones, then sat outside by the river and watched the fireworks. Looked pretty cozy to me."

My eyes had to be bulging from their sockets. Dad had a date? Why did he not tell us?

After she handed Brandon his order, she rang them up and Brandon paid; however, before he could pull his hand back from getting his change, Mrs. Jennings wrapped her hand as much as she could around his bicep. "Some men stop working out when they leave the Army. You're still as built as the day you returned."

He cleared his throat. "Thank you." The words came out strangled, and I had to press my lips together to keep from falling over in gales of laughter. "Do you want to take a walk?" His eyes pleaded with me to say yes, but something in me couldn't let him get off so easily.

"Maybe we should sit down and finish our ice cream first?"

"Oh, honey, don't be such a spoilsport," said Mrs. Jennings. "It's a gorgeous night, and if you walk down the path towards the woods, you might see some lightning bugs. I've seen more this year than I have in a long while. That pond down there is quite romantic already, but those lightning bugs really create an atmosphere, I tell you."

I lifted one shoulder in a sort of half-hearted shrug. "I suppose." Yes, the tone was overdramatic, but Brandon's expression made every bit of my little act worth it.

"Don't put yourself out."

I could barely hold in the snort that threatened to escape when his eyes narrowed and his voice rumbled in that low baritone. "Come on. Let's go." I motioned toward the door with my head and smiled at Mrs. Jennings. "Thanks, Mrs. J. Take care!"

"Don't do anything I wouldn't do, my dears!"

Brandon nearly choked on his ice cream as we emerged from the air conditioning into the warm humidity outside. "I can't believe you."

The evil cackle I'd been holding in finally rang out across the water, startling a duck swimming near the shore. "That was fun. I haven't seen you squirm like that since Carrie Bridley tried to corner you at the eighth grade Valentine's dance."

"But you saved me that time. You didn't conspire against me."

"Mrs. Jennings is harmless. She's just an old lady who likes to flirt with all you young bucks who come into her shop."

"Young buck?" One side of his lips quirked upwards. "You think I'm a young buck?"

"I didn't say that." I took a lick along the side of my cone where it threatened to drip down my fingers. "But, I'm willing to wager Mrs. Jennings thinks you are."

"I'll get you back for that."

With a roll of my eyes, I flicked my hair over my shoulder. "Promises, promises."

As I turned, a spring came into my step while I followed the riverside walkway. I loved this part of town. Before we moved into the house, I lived in a tiny studio over one of the shops lining the river. The apartment boasted a large window overlooking the water—the best part of the place in my opinion. I kept a small table in front of it so I could eat my breakfast and drink my coffee or tea while I watched the walkway come alive. Every morning, the ducks woke, pulling their heads from under their downy wings before they swam around the river, dunking their heads in search of food.

Brandon's long legs helped him catch up to my side as we continued down the path. Only the restaurant, Riverfront, sat on the other side of the river near the bridge, so once you passed the ice cream parlor, the opposite side was forest with great oaks and Spanish moss that, in places, hung low over the water. At twilight, those gnarled-looking oak limbs with their trailing adornments cast long, dark shadows with the setting sun. If only it were earlier in the year and the cicadas were still out—that would complete the atmosphere.

I tossed my napkin into the last trash can before the end of the paved path, and we continued further along toward the absolute end where the water bubbled down a rocky section of riverbed. It wasn't terribly dark, yet in the pitch-black recesses of the trees, I could see the small flashes of yellow from the lightning bugs.

When I lived just down the path, I loved to come at night and see if the lightning bugs were out. They reminded me of summer nights when I was a girl, eating watermelon on our back porch while those little lights flickered in the trees, not to mention Daddy catching one in a Mason jar for us to get a closer look.

"Look at that," said Brandon in a murmur. "I haven't seen that many in a long time. I wonder why there's so many this year."

"I don't know. I wonder if Daddy has any in the backyard."

"Daddy?"

I looked up as he turned toward me, our eyes catching. "I was just remembering when we were kids," I said with a shrug. "I guess it slipped out."

One side of his lips curved. "You have ice cream on the edge of your mouth."

"Where?"

His fingers reached to softly brush near my lip. I couldn't pull my eyes from him while he wiped the last of the bubblegum from my face. I stood stock still. I couldn't move. What the holy heck? His gaze shifted from my lips to lock with mine, and my mouth was so dry, I may as well have been sucking on a sponge. I licked my lips in the hopes it would help, but it only made things dreadfully worse. The air crackled with a current I'd never noticed before, prickling my skin and making goosebumps break out down my back. His head dipped a hairsbreadth, and I jumped.

"Are you ready to go?" I took one last glimpse into the trees where the lightning bugs still blinked away, oblivious to my temporary insanity. What was wrong with me? This was Brandon—dependable, big brother-type Brandon. I clutched my arms to my sides as I started to walk back, perhaps more briskly than our trip down the path.

"Jena? Are you okay?"

"Yes," I said, wincing at how high-pitched my voice sounded. "I'm fine. Why?"

I wouldn't be reacting to him this way if it weren't for Ellie. She had to overanalyze our friendship and make me question everything. Now, I couldn't get comfortable around him, not really. I dragged in a breath, filling my lungs with air, and released it slowly. I was going to kill her.

"Are you sure you're okay?"

"Yes, I'm just tired. I think it's time to go home."

Chapter 4

I had time before the oncoming car would even come close, so I jogged as gracefully as I could in three-inch heels across the street. I'd just met with a couple at the Methodist Church and needed to get back to work before another meeting with a client at one.

My foot had barely hit the sidewalk when my cell phone vibrated in my palm. Without checking to see who was calling, I touched the screen and put it to my ear. "Jena Barrett."

"Why are you avoiding me?" Brandon's deep voice sent a jolt rippling through my body, and I halted in my footsteps. "I've been trying to call you for the last week and a half, and you're not answering your phone. I knocked on your door last weekend, and you didn't answer."

"That must have been when I had dinner with my dad. I'm not avoiding you."

"Uh-huh."

"I did!" I bit the inside of my cheek as I started walking again. I was *so* lying! After that disturbing night at the movies, I needed time to forget Ellie's absolutely ludicrous suspicions and get back to my normal self around him. I just couldn't see how I could do that when we were together so often. So, when he'd tried to call me, I'd texted him back later and made up some excuse—I was with a client, a vendor, in the shower or bath, etcetera, etcetera. I winced. Lord, I was a terrible friend.

"Am I still your date for Ellie's wedding?" he asked, interrupting me scolding myself. "I have my own invitation so if you'd rather not—"

"Yes, of course you are. I'm sorry. It's been crazy lately." I stopped in my tracks once again. Unless . . . "Did you have someone else you wanted to take? If you do, it's not a problem." It wasn't like it was a *real* date. We often went as the other's plus one.

"No, I haven't asked anyone else nor am I looking to. It's a family wedding. I wouldn't ask a woman I wasn't seriously dating."

He had a point. Our families had always been close. He thought of Ellie as a little sister and he'd become good friends with William, who'd asked Brandon to be a groomsman. Brandon wouldn't bring a casual fling or budding relationship. "Sorry. I hadn't thought about it that way."

"It's okay. I'll pick you up at five on Friday, so we can catch the last boat out to the island. Maybe then you can tell me what I've done to piss you off."

"You haven't pissed me off."

"Could've fooled me."

"Brandon," I said, drawing out his name. "I—"

"I'm sorry, Jena. I can't right now. I have two patients waiting on me, but I didn't want to wait until the last minute to get in touch with you. Mrs. Bertram is here with that little, bad-tempered pug nightmare, and you know how grouchy she can get."

"The woman or the dog?"

A snort came through the earpiece. "Ha ha. Both."

"See you Friday."

"Bye."

The line clicked before I could say goodbye. Crud! It was Tuesday, so I had to figure something out or purge whatever stupid switch Ellie'd flipped in my brain before Friday. If I kept being such a colossal idiot around him, I'd lose my best friend, which could not happen. I had three days to solve the problem. I could do it! I would do it!

I glanced around me. Had I said that out loud? The entire town would be gossiping that I'd lost my mind if someone heard me. It was all I could do not to groan. How did I get myself into these messes?

My clients were sitting in the waiting room when I reached the office. I wish I could say I was one hundred percent present for that meeting, but I couldn't stop thinking about Brandon's phone call. How was I supposed to explain what insanity came on so suddenly? I couldn't understand what was happening myself, much less make it a coherent thought. And what could possibly make up for not calling him for almost two weeks?

When the client meeting finished, I hurried upstairs and changed into my denim cut-offs, a white top, and my light striped cardigan. Once I'd thrown on my Converse, I jumped into my car and headed toward the highway. Maybe a long drive would purge this mess from my head. I drove down the coast for probably an hour until I turned around and headed back toward Marysville. The next thing I knew, I found myself sitting in my dad's driveway.

I watched the house for a while. If asked, I couldn't have told you how long or even why, but I sat in my car until I nearly jumped out of my seat at a loud knock on the window.

"Are you going to sit out here all evening, or do you want to come in?" My dad chuckled when I opened the door. "Sorry about scaring you. I didn't realize your mind was somewhere else."

"It's okay."

"Come on in." He waved me toward the house as he began to stroll in that direction. "I'll pour us a glass of whiskey, and we'll talk. You look like you could use it."

"I don't know if I want to talk, Daddy."

He turned with his bushy eyebrows lifted high on his forehead. "Daddy? This must be serious. You girls haven't called me that in over a decade."

"It's not serious."

His eyes held mine for a moment before his lips gave a slight twitch. "Nice try, but I don't believe you."

I walked inside the small two-bedroom house he'd purchased after the divorce from my mother. When I walked into the living room, I stopped and gawked at the unusual sight in front of me. "Dad, when did you buy a sofa and end tables?" Unlike the home where I grew up, this one never possessed dainty feminine touches or true decoration. No pictures adorned the walls. In fact, nothing but my father's recliner, television, household appliances, and bedroom suite usually took up space within those sparse walls, which was why he always visited us at our houses. Now, he had actual furniture and even a painting hanging over the mantel. Since when did my father buy art?

He scratched the back of his neck while he squinted at the sofa. "A month ago?" He pointed his finger in the direction of the kitchen. "Whiskey."

I followed him through and scanned the room while he pulled a bottle out of a bottom cabinet and poured a finger into two glasses. A bowl of fruit lay on the counter, no pizza boxes were stacked by the trash can, and the place was spotless. I swear you could've eaten off the floors.

"Dad? What's going on?"

"What do you mean?" He handed me my drink and watched me while he took a sip.

"Well, when you divorced Mom, you took the spare bedroom set, your recliner, and the living room TV. You purchased a refrigerator as well as a washer and dryer, but you've never seen fit to buy more furniture until now. There's an actual painting over the fireplace.

"You've existed on takeout and grilled steak despite Ellie's and my efforts to persuade you otherwise. The house is never this clean." I pointed to the trash can. "There are no pizza boxes. There's a fruit bowl, Dad, and unless I'm hallucinating, it has apples and bananas in it." Like a light bulb, a memory popped into my head. "Mrs. Jennings also may have mentioned a few weeks ago that you brought a woman into her shop."

"Gossiping old biddy," he muttered.

"Of course she is, but you still took your date there for ice cream." I followed him through the sliding glass door to the patio. "Are you seeing someone, and if so, why are you hiding it from me and Ellie?"

A low growl I'd never heard came from him. "I haven't dated for thirty years. I thought we could get to know each other. I wanted to see how things went before I introduced her to you girls."

"Is it serious?"

He gave a non-committal shrug while he looked out over the large backyard. "I see her nearly every day. She comes over and cooks a good bit. I took her to the student art exhibit on campus. That's where I bought the painting."

That explained the fruit bowl and the immaculate kitchen. Had she managed to get Dad to actually eat fruit? He was a notorious steak and potatoes kind of guy.

"We watch TV and movies a lot."

"Have you taken her to Bingo night yet?"

His head shot up. "I've never gone to Bingo night and you know it. No woman is going to get me to Bingo night. I'd rather shoot myself in the foot."

I giggled and took a sip of my drink, flinching at the sting as it went down my throat. "Just checking. If you actually went, then I'd know you'd lost your mind."

"Hardy, har, har."

"How long has this been going on?"

He took a sip of his whiskey and bared his teeth as he swallowed. "Three months."

"I can't believe you never told us! Dad! How could you?"

"Oh, please! Like Ellie told me about William before Freya was born, or you told me about your boyfriends. That's hypocritical."

"Okay." I held up a hand, palm out. "You're right. I'm sorry."

After a nod, he leaned back in the seat. "So, are you going to tell me what has your panties in a bunch?"

"Do I have to?" I stared into my glass like it was the most interesting thing on the planet.

"Won't do much good to hold it in. Besides, it's not like I'm going to say anything to anyone."

I scrunched up my nose and lips. "I have this friend."

"A friend, huh?"

At his dry tone, I looked at him and straightened, daring him to challenge me. "Yes, a friend. She's been best friends with someone since—well, for as long as she can remember. Someone suggested to her that this 'friend' might be more than a 'friend,' and now, it has her seriously confused."

His eyebrows drew together in the middle and he frowned. "Confused how?"

"This man has always been there, and she's always been comfortable with him, but lately, she's nervous and jittery. She even avoided him for a couple of weeks, hoping it would all go away."

A long exhale filled the momentary silence. "Has it gone away?"

"Not really."

He glanced over at the trees to the back of the lot and then back to me, crossing one ankle over the opposite knee. "The way I see it, you need to figure out whether you want Brandon to remain nothing more than your friend or whether that nervous, jittery feeling you're getting means the two of you should be more than friends."

"I never said this was about me and Brandon."

"You didn't have to, sweetheart," he said with a crusty laugh. "I've wondered for years whether that boy would get off his ass and ask you on a real date. Whatever you do, be careful with him. I suspect he's been harboring some serious feelings for you for a long time. You don't want to hurt him."

I downed the rest of my drink and set my glass on the brick planter next to me. "I don't know what I want. How am I supposed to figure that out?"

"Time."

"That's a crappy answer."

"It's the best I can do," he responded. "You need to decide if what you're feeling is more than a brotherly sort of love and whether you have the guts to go for it. It's riskier than dating a man you met at one of your weddings or at a club. This is your best friend. Your relationship will never be the same whether you succeed or whether you fail. Are you willing to risk that?"

"You sound like you're trying to scare me off."

His head gave an almost imperceptible shake. "Not at all. I think a relationship with him could be the best thing that ever happens to you, but it's not my decision to make. It's yours."

"There you are." We both turned to where a woman emerged from the side of the house, a bag of groceries in one hand.

"Sorry!" My dad sprang from his chair and hurried over to take the bag. "Jena came over for a chat, so we came out here." He gave her a quick kiss on the cheek before he glanced back at me. "Melanie, this is my oldest, Jena. Jena, this is Melanie."

I stood and stepped forward with my hand out. "It's nice to meet you."

"It's wonderful to finally meet you," she said with a Southern drawl as big as her smile. "Your dad talks about you and your sister all of the time. He's so proud of the two of you. I've been looking forward to meeting you for a while."

My father turned a few shades of red while I simply smiled and nodded. "I'm glad Dad has found a . . . friend." I had no idea what else to call her. It wasn't like he'd told me whether or not they were an actual item. I pointed to the bag of groceries. "You have plans. I should go."

"Oh! You don't have to leave," said Melanie quickly. "Tom, tell her she doesn't need to leave." Her hand took mine. "I brought plenty of food. I was going to make shrimp over zucchini noodles. It's nothing fancy but I'd love to get to know you better."

Dad gave a dry chuckle and slid open the sliding glass door. "Jena, I'm sure you don't have to run off so soon."

"There!" said Melanie, triumphantly. "See, you should stay." I didn't get a word out before I was led into the cool air of the house and pressed toward a stool. When had Dad bought barstools for the kitchen?

I watched Melanie as she unloaded the bag onto the counter. If I had to guess her age, I'd say she was in her fifties, even though she looked more like mid-forties. Her dark mahogany ponytail looped down into a curl at the end. She didn't wear much makeup, just enough to highlight her features, and she dressed in a cute shorts outfit, showing off a pretty nice pair of legs for a woman her age. She had to exercise. Dad never exercised.

"So, how did the two of you meet?" I peered back and forth between them.

"I met your dad on campus." She paused removing items from the bag and lifted her hands that she used to gesture while she spoke.

"Are you a professor as well?"

She laughed cheerfully. "Oh, honey, no, I'm a master's student in the English department, studying English literature—more specifically, the Romantic poets."

My eyes stretched as they widened at my father. "You're dating a student? Isn't that frowned upon or something?" Melanie giggled while my dad rolled his eyes.

"I'm in the history department, remember?" he said in a flat tone. "I have nothing to do with Melanie's degree and she isn't and won't be in any of my classes."

"Heavens, no!" Melanie stuck out her tongue and crinkled her nose. "I have no desire to take a class on the American Civil War or your father's intersession class on the Kennedy Assassination. I hear enough over dinner some nights."

I glanced over at my father to find him smiling crookedly at the woman with this puppy dog expression. He never looked at my mom that way, or if he did, it was long before I could remember. He had it bad, but then Melanie must truly like him to listen to him drone on about his two favorite subjects and classes.

"I know your young man, you know?"

My head whipped back to look at Melanie. "I'm sorry. Who?"

She shrugged while she rummaged in a cabinet. "I suppose since the two of you aren't together, I shouldn't call him your young man, but from what your father has told me, he *is* your best friend."

"Brandon?" Shoot me now! I'd actually managed to put him from my mind for an entire two seconds before Melanie managed to drag him right back, front and center. How did she know him?

"Yes, that's him. He's so handsome with that sandy hair and the light coating of stubble on his face. I don't think I've ever seen such amazing hazel eyes before. The color reminds me of cured tobacco." He must've been wearing brown. His eyes almost appeared to have a different hue depending upon the color of his shirt. Some shades made them appear greener.

"I wouldn't call him my young man. He can date whomever he wants."

She sighed as she placed a pan on the stove. "Such a shame. You know, I grew up with these two who were inseparable when they were young. They dated other people during high school but became an item during college. I believe they've been married thirty years now—and they have five children." My dad began to cough and splutter, his whiskey glass hitting the bar with a clunk.

"Dad? Are you okay?"

He nodded and waved his hand at me. "I'm fine," he managed to croak out. "Last of the whiskey went down the wrong way." His voice cleared the more he spoke.

A glass of water appeared in front of him. "This might help." Melanie moved the whiskey glass back to the counter.

"Thank you." He took a few sips and patted my hand. "See, all better."

I relaxed back into my seat and steeled myself. "Dad, are you bringing Melanie to Ellie's wedding?"

The next thing I knew he dissolved into another fit of coughs, clunking the water glass on the bar and turning crimson in the process. I slapped him on the back until he could get himself back under control.

"I don't think your father wanted to spring me on the two of you on such a big day," said Melanie, watching Dad while she turned on the gas burner. Her eyebrows were drawn together, and she frowned. "Are you okay, Tom?"

"Yes, I promise." He cleared his throat one more time. "I thought it might be too much of a shock when the two of you hadn't met her."

Melanie added some oil to the pan while she scrunched one side of her face. "I don't know. I wouldn't want to take any of the spotlight from the bride or take away from her day."

"I don't think it would be a problem—if Dad wants to bring you and you want to come, that is." The two of them turned and regarded one another for a moment while I sat back and relaxed. I'd managed to change the subject away from Brandon—not that I'd discovered how Melanie knew him. One thing was certain, I wasn't going to bring it up now. Maybe I could hide away from him for a little longer? Who was I kidding? If Melanie didn't bring him up again, my traitorous mind would at some point. At least I wasn't dreaming about him! Oh, crap! Why did I have to go and give myself that idea?

Chapter 5

With an exaggerated groan, Brandon heaved my bags into the back of his SUV. "We're only going for the weekend. Did you have to pack your entire closet?"

I paused as I passed him and propped my hands on my hips. "I didn't pack my entire closet. I have my dress and shoes for tonight, my clothes for the breakfast in the morning, my dress and shoes for the wedding, makeup, hair dryer, brush, pajamas, and clothes for coming home on Sunday."

"Right, your entire closet." He winked with a wicked grin.

I gave a huff. "You're being ridiculous. I can lift my own suitcase, so it's not that heavy. You're insufferable sometimes."

"Please! You love me because I'm insufferable. Besides, you can be just as ornery when you're in the right mood."

"Takes one to know one," I said in a sing-song voice like when we were kids. I stuck out my tongue and jumped into the car before he could retaliate.

When the door opened, he climbed in, shaking his head and laughing. "First, you try to hand me over to Mrs. Jennings like a lobster on a silver platter, and now this. You forget that payback is a bitch."

"Language, Mr. Taylor." After I buckled my seatbelt, I rotated a bit to face him. "And your paybacks are never as bad as you seem to think."

He waggled his eyebrows. "That's because I've never followed through on some of my more heinous plans."

"Like?"

He rested his forearm on the center console, facing me head on. "Like giving your phone number to Creeper Collins. You know he's wanted to ask you out since middle school."

I gasped and punched him in the bicep. "That's worse than anything I've ever done to you."

"I know. I've never done it, have I?" He rubbed his arm, then grabbed my hand. "I admit that I've been tempted a number of times, though."

His warmth seeped into my palm, so I shook his hand off. I couldn't let him touch me if I kept getting all tingly and twitchy when he did—not if I was going to figure out what this mess meant. "Get driving. I don't want to be late for the rehearsal dinner."

"Now, who's being ridiculous. We have hours." He started the car and pulled from the curb. "You're the one who wanted to arrive right at check-in time, remember? You probably intend on reapplying an entire new face of make-up."

My back stiffened. "I don't wear that much."

"No, you don't, but you don't need the stuff at all. You're still drop-dead gorgeous without a stitch of concealer or powder or whatever else you wear." While he spoke, he glanced in my direction with a completely serious look.

"What do you want?" I lifted my eyebrows and watched him. He'd told me on more than one occasion that I didn't require make-up. Why flatter me like this? He never did that. What was that about?

"What do you mean?"

"I'm drop-dead gorgeous? Really?"

With a shrug, he gripped the steering wheel a bit tighter. "Am I not allowed to say that? Does it break the best friend code or something?"

"Best friend code?" I said, with a bark of a laugh.

"Yes, like you could never date my brother, or I could never date your sister. You know, stuff like that."

"You wanted to date my sister?" I had to press my lips together to keep from giggling. I knew what his reaction would be, and it didn't disappoint.

His lips puckered and he shook his head vehemently. "You know Ellie is like a little sister to me! Eww, why?"

"Because you deserved it." I couldn't help but grin as I settled back for the drive. Brandon turned on some music, and we chitchatted about random nothingness when the mood struck us. I don't know when I started staring at him, but during one of the lulls in conversation, I didn't turn back to the road in front of us but continued to watch Brandon—the set of his jaw, the light spattering of stubble on his cheek from not shaving that morning, the way his thick eyelashes framed his eyes. I was tracing the lush line of his bottom lip when it curved.

"What are you doing?"

My insides jumped. I looked back out the front window as we pulled into the marina parking lot. "What do you mean?"

"You were staring."

"I zoned out. Sorry."

He parked before he turned and caught my eye. "Are you sure that's all?"

"Positive." I was so lying! It was all I could do to keep from looking for that lightning bolt from the heavens that would strike me down where I sat. When I bolstered enough courage to take a glimpse in his direction, a slight glint of something in his eyes told me he didn't believe me, but he didn't say it. Instead, he simply got out of the car and moved around the back to unload our luggage.

The boat service the resort provided from the marina only lasted about thirty minutes. We couldn't talk over the noise from the boat and the wind while we traveled, and Brandon helped me unload my bag when we arrived. When we stepped up to the front counter of the hotel lobby, the young woman at the computer tilted her head coyly, smiling at Brandon. "May I help you, sir?"

Good grief! She might as well have written "screw me" on her forehead with that expression.

"Reservation for Barrett," he said pointing at me, "and a reservation for Taylor."

After clicking a few keys, the lady's face brightened. "Ellie Barrett? The bride?"

I took a step closer and set my hand on the high counter. "No, I'm her sister. The reservation should be under Jena, though Ellie did make it with her own."

The young woman clicked a few more keys. "I don't have a Jena Barrett. I'm sorry." My spine went rigid, but Brandon spoke before I could become testy.

"What about Brandon Taylor?"

She typed and started to nod, practically batting her eyelashes when she looked up at Brandon. I bit the inside of my cheek. "Yes, I do have one for Brandon Taylor."

"Do you have a free room for this weekend?" I asked, hopefully.

Her smile disappeared when she glanced at me. "I'm sorry, miss. We're all booked up. Aside from the wedding, we have a publishers' conference checking in tonight. However, I can take your name in the event someone cancels."

Brandon peered at me and fished out his wallet from his back pocket. "Will my room accommodate more than one person, and if so, how much extra?"

The young woman, Misty according to her name tag, glanced between us. "Yes, the room has a super king-sized bed and can accommodate two people. There's no extra fee for two on that room, and we have your credit card on file from the initial reservation. It's all taken care of."

Share a room with Brandon? With my recent fixation on him, I couldn't sleep with him as I had before. What if I talked in my sleep? Oh, Lord, what if I groped him? "I can stay with Charlie." The words came out rushed and clipped. I resisted the urge to wince.

Brandon turned back to me with his eyebrows lifted as high as they could go. "You never want to sleep with Charlie. She snores, remember?"

Crap! I'd forgotten about that! "Well, Ellie might not stay with William tonight. Seeing the bride before the wedding and all that. I can stay with her." I avoided looking him in the eye. He'd know I'd lost my mind if I did.

His eyes narrowed a hairsbreadth while he put away his credit card. "I've never known Ellie to be superstitious."

I glanced at his shoulder. I couldn't handle much more. "She mentioned she might just for fun. We didn't have a bachelorette party, so we might have a pajama party."

As Misty handed him his keycard, I didn't miss that one of her fingers brushed his hand—the little hussy. However, he didn't react and, in fact, appeared oblivious as he thanked her and shoved the plastic card into his pocket. I reached for my suitcase, but before I could wrap my greedy fingers around the handle, Brandon grabbed it and began rolling it down the hall.

"What are you doing?" I hurried after him while he continued briskly, taking a turn and heading to the ground floor suites that overlooked the beach. At the very last door, he slipped the card in the slot and entered, pushing our luggage against the wall. "I can stay with Ellie," I said insistently, trailing after him. "What are you doing?"

When he turned around, he crossed his arms over his chest. "What's going on?" His voice held a bite it normally didn't have, and this time, I did balk slightly. I never liked that voice—not that he'd used it with me often.

I scraped my teeth along my bottom lip. "I don't know what you mean."

"Bull shit."

"Language, Taylor." He knew I didn't like cussing.

"I don't care," he replied without a pause. "You've never had an issue staying with me or me staying with you until now. Something's up, and I'm tired of being avoided over whatever is going on with you. I want to know what it is. Have I done something to upset you?"

I shoved my hands into the pockets of my white Capri pants, my shoulders tightened, and I searched frantically for the right words. "Nothing is up." Fail! That wouldn't stop him.

"You're lying." He pointed directly at my chest, his body bent slightly forward. "You're lying. That little crease between your eyebrows gives you away. You've been hiding from me for the last few weeks, and you're sidestepping the issue even now. I'm not playing this guessing game anymore. We've been best friends since we were practically born. I deserve to know what's going on."

While he spoke, I covered my face with my hands in an attempt to calm myself. Confrontation was my mortal enemy. I avoided it like brussels sprouts and the plague. The last thing in the world I wanted to do was hurt him, but that last bit of sanity hung on by a thread that snapped when he raised his voice. "Because I need space!"

He recoiled like I'd delivered a stinging slap and stepped back. "From me? Why?"

"It's so stupid," I said, almost at a whisper.

"It can't be that stupid if you're letting it come between us."

My eyes trained on this spot on the wall over his shoulder and blinked rapidly. I couldn't look at him. Why couldn't I hold his eye while I explained? "Ellie said something, and it's just stuck in my head. I need time to clear it."

"What did she say?" Why wouldn't his voice lose that edge, the one that hinted of his impatience and anger? Regardless of how much I tried to play this down, that didn't ease.

"It's not important." I pulled my hands from my pockets and stared at them, my fingers fidgeting.

"Jena, please." His voice had become plaintive and pulled my eyes to his. "I want to understand what's happening."

I sucked a deep breath into my lungs in an attempt to stop myself from shaking. "Ellie suggested that you don't date because you have feelings for me. She also said that my terrible taste in men is because subconsciously, I have feelings for you."

He shoved his hands into his pockets and walked past me to look out of the window. "Would it bother you if I cared for you as more than a friend?" His tone softened, thank goodness, but something unfamiliar lurked there as well.

"I don't know. At times, it does. I don't want to lose you. What would I do without you?"

He nodded and turned around. "But you might not lose me."

"What?" Something jerked in my chest and twisted. Ellie couldn't be right. Not about him at least!

He lifted his hand from his pocket, and as he approached, he brushed a few tendrils of hair that had fallen out of my ponytail away from my face, tucking them behind my ear. Those same fingers drifted from my hair to cradle the back of my neck as everything around us faded and my breathing quickened. "What if we could be best friends for the rest of our lives?"

I swallowed and licked my impossibly dry lips. "We will be, won't we? We agreed when we were ten remember?"

One side of his full lips curved upward, and suddenly I was short of breath. "When we were ten," he said, "I envisioned us merely older but still roaming in the woods and camping out together. It was a child's fantasy, but I'm not a boy anymore, and that isn't what I've wanted for some time now."

Those hazel eyes held mine and wouldn't let go as his face dipped ever so slightly. We may as well have stood in an ice-cold meat locker my body shook so hard, and my heart thrummed against my ribs in this crazy staccato beat. I gasped and stepped back. "I'm sorry. I can't. I need some air."

Before he could say a word, I jetted through the door and slammed the bar open to the nearest exit. I rushed toward the water, stopping just before the sand changed from the clean, bleach white to the damp darker portion where the water flowed up over the beach and receded, venturing back out to parts unknown.

Footsteps approached from behind, and I didn't need to peer over my shoulder to know it was Brandon. When he stood beside me, I continued to gaze out over the crystal blue waves. "How long?" How had Ellie known? More importantly, how had I missed the change in our relationship—the change on his side anyway?

"Have I felt more?" he asked, making me nod. "Definitely since I returned from vet school, but I think I began to fall in love with you while I was in the Army."

The Army? When I turned, he wasn't watching me but still faced the ocean, his hands in his pockets.

"When I was at basic training, the letters you wrote kept me going when I thought it would never end, when I thought I wouldn't make it through. During those four years, we called, we emailed, we exchanged letters and postcards. I confided everything to you. I poured all my hopes and dreams into each and every word. I didn't realize at the time how much it all meant, not until I came home and laid eyes upon your face again. You know me better than anyone, even my parents."

"But you never said a word."

The gold flecks in his hazel eyes glimmered in the bright sun. "I knew you didn't feel the same. I believed that over time my infatuation with you would fade—that we could return to how our friendship was before. Instead, those feelings have only grown deeper, so instead, I started hoping you might have your own revelation. I've wanted you to love me as much as I love you." He glanced out over the water and back. "Do you know how long Ellie's suspected?"

I shook my head. "She never said."

"Is this why you've been avoiding me?"

All I could do was nod and dig my teeth into my bottom lip. I could be such a ninny, and this was one of those moments.

"Why? Was the idea of falling in love with me that terrible?"

"No! If I ever felt anything more than friendship, I never recognized it for what it was. Since Ellie mentioned it, the idea of our relationship changing has freaked me out. It scares me to death." I don't know why I rubbed my arms like I was cold; the weather was warm.

"You don't think it scares me too?" His head tilted in more. The air around us prickled at my skin like it carried some strange electrical charge, and it also became hard to breathe. "You don't know how many times I've almost told you. I'd fight to get those words to the tip of my tongue, and you'd say or do something to make me swallow them back down. It's why I waited for some sign from you; otherwise, I was afraid you'd turn tail and run."

"Like I did today." Before my fingers could snatch that lock of hair the breeze pulled across my face, Brandon combed it back from my cheek.

"Yeah, like you did today. Charlie kept bugging me to finally—"

"Charlie knows?"

"She figured it out. Now that I think about it, I must've been crap at hiding my feelings."

"It explains why Charlie never liked Connor."

One side of his lips quirked up. "She didn't like Connor because he's an asshole, not because of me. She blamed me for my own heartache. As far as she was concerned, I should've told you what was in my heart a long time ago." Charlie had always had that practical streak. She would see things that way.

At his exhale, my eyes returned to his. "I understand if you want to sleep with Charlie or Ellie," he said. "But, if you need a place to stay, I promise not to push you. I'll let you sleep, even if it's torture."

My head gave a slight hitch to one side. "Is it? Torture, I mean?"

"Sometimes. Particularly when you've been drinking and beg me for help removing your clothes. Fourth of July nearly killed me. You've soundly managed on more than one occasion to turn parts of my anatomy a painful blue."

My cheeks radiated heat, and I grazed my teeth along my lip.

"And you've got to stop that with all of the licking and biting your lips," he said with a groan.

"I'm sorry." I pressed my lips together tightly.

With a sigh, he took my hand and pulled me into his arms. "No, I'm sorry. I know you're not intentionally teasing me. It's just that when you bite or lick your lips, I want to throw you down on the sand and kiss you until you forget every doubt in that pretty little head of yours."

His breath tickled my ear, creating a wave of goosebumps down my spine while I rose to my tiptoes and wrapped my arms around his neck. Before I was ready, he kissed my cheek and pulled away. "Let's go back to the room and wait for everyone else. I'm sure your sister will be here soon enough and will probably have a few choice words for the resort about your missing room."

I could just see Ellie at the counter, letting her pregnancy hormones run rampant on poor Misty. If I hadn't minded the way Misty'd eyed Brandon like a lollipop, I might've felt sorry for the poor girl, but as it stood, I kind of wanted to watch Ellie reduce Misty to a blubbering mess. How wrong was that? I was all but terrified of committing to a relationship or any sort of romantic feelings with Brandon, but I was jealous of someone he'd only just met and virtually ignored the advances of for the five minutes they interacted. Good grief! I needed therapy!

Chapter 6

The rehearsal and dinner went off without a hitch. We ate outside on the patio of the restaurant with candles and oil lamps helping to illuminate the tables. Between Ellie's happiness and the pregnancy, my little sister glowed from her place at the center of the table, and for such a reticent man, William wore the most animated smile I'd ever seen. I'd always been content with my life, but lately, I'd been envious of Ellie's amazing luck in finding the perfect man for her. I'd turned thirty-two in February. Would I ever have the happiness she now held firmly in her grasp? Was Brandon whom I'd been searching for all along?

Brandon remained close by for the evening, as usual, remaining the all-around perfect date. He hadn't mentioned our conversation earlier on the beach. He hadn't behaved at all out of the ordinary, but regardless, he drove me batty. He brought me glasses of wine, he joked and conversed with my family like he was one of them, and he sat next to me during the meal. All of those things were nothing, yet they were everything.

His fingers brushed mine when he handed me a glass of Malbec, making the hair on my arms prickle. His low chuckle vibrated down my spine and did funny things to my tummy and further down . . . I swear my thighs squeezed tighter together when he laughed at a bawdy joke my dad made. The light hand on my back when I entered through the door before him tickled in a way it never had before. Was this normal or my imagination? I'd never had someone elicit such a physical response from me before, especially in such simple ways.

At the end of the night, we'd had no pajama party. Ellie could barely keep her eyes open by the time William wanted to return to their room—Brandon had been correct. Ellie hadn't booked a room for herself that night. She hadn't wanted to spend even one night without William, so he whisked her away to their suite where Freya had already gone to bed hours earlier with a sitter they'd hired for the weekend.

Now, what felt like hours later, I stared at Charlie, lying beside me with her mouth wide open and a resonating snore that would inevitably shake the bed. Even in the dark room, a slight glistening of drool shone from her cheek. A bright red two o'clock glared from the bedside alarm clock. I sighed. I couldn't be up all night!

Carefully, I pulled the covers back from me and inched my legs over the side. I'd never get any sleep if I stayed here. The problem would be Brandon's smug face when I showed up at his door, but at this rate, I'd deal with him giving me grief for a month if I could get a minuscule five minutes of uninterrupted sleep!

I slipped on my Converse, grabbed my make-up bag from the bathroom, and zipped up my suitcase as quietly as I could, watching Charlie the entire time. As soon as the wheels of my luggage hit the floor, I sidled through the door and cushioned it closed behind me.

Luckily, no one walked the halls so late. Even so, when I stepped onto the elevator, a woman gave me an odd look. I must've looked strange in my pajama shorts and tank-top with all of my belongings either pulled behind me or in my hand.

When I reached Brandon's door, I knocked as quietly as I could and waited. After a few minutes, I leaned against the wall and took out my cell phone, texting in the hopes the chime or vibration might wake him. Finally, I pulled up his number and hit send. I dropped my head against the wall and waited, trying not to fall asleep where I stood. The door whipped open a moment later, making me jump away from my comfortable spot.

"You finally had enough?" A smile stole across his face, not that I looked at his face for too long. His hair was adorably mussed, but my eyes didn't stay on his hair either. My gaze traced down to his broad shoulders and his well-defined pecs, which boasted a spattering of hair in the middle that trailed down to his six-pack abs. His cotton shorts rode low on his hips and my eyes froze on that line of hair that disappeared under the waistband.

"Jena," he said, his voice dangerously low. "Unless you want to do something besides sleep, you need to stop looking at me like that."

He took the makeup bag from my hand and my suitcase handle to pull it into the room while I followed dumbly behind him, now staring at the muscles shift in his back deliciously as he moved. What was going on with me? It wasn't like I'd never seen him without a shirt. Were my hormones in overdrive?

"I don't know if I can sleep here either." I crossed my arms over my chest in case my nipples were poking out and saying "hi." The room was dimly lit by the bathroom light, but they might be noticeable. I had no way of knowing without drawing attention to them.

"Stop thinking so much. You've got to be exhausted. I know I am."

"That's because I woke you up."

Brandon grabbed my hand and pulled me toward the bed, turning off the light on the way. "Just lie down. I'm willing to bet you'll be out before you know it."

I crawled under the covers where he'd pulled them back to get up and settled in on my side. The mattress shifted when he followed, but he didn't cuddle up to me like he usually did. Instead, his breathing filled the silence rather than Charlie's sonorous snores. He was trying to make me more comfortable, and I loved him for it.

"Brandon?"

"Yeah?"

I reached back and took his hand, pulling him toward me. "I miss you." He pressed up against my back with his hand wrapped around my stomach, but something I never noticed before pressed hard against my rear. "Is that what I think it is?"

"Ignore him. I can't help it that he likes you . . . a lot. He'll go away after a while."

"Are you sure?"

His lips pressed against my shoulder. "Are you offering?"

My insides flipped and squirmed. "I feel like a tease. I could find somewhere else."

"Go to sleep, Jena. I can wait until you're ready. I know you're more than worth it."

His fingers laced with mine, and I laid there, listening to his breathing change and eventually become more even, indicating he'd fallen asleep. Other things eventually fell asleep also and faded. I sighed and relaxed into his embrace until I was blissfully unaware of everything around me.

Gentle fingers combed through my hair as I sighed and relaxed, not yet opening my eyes. Brandon's chest rose and fell under my cheek. My arm was wrapped around his torso as I shifted my leg, the hair on his thigh rubbing along mine.

"Good morning," he said in a soft murmur, his lips planting a soft kiss on my forehead. "I hope you slept okay."

"Much better. I had forgotten how bad Charlie snores."

His chest shook as I opened my eyes. He rolled to his side, so we faced each other, our heads sharing a pillow. "What time is the bridesmaids' breakfast?"

"Brunch. It's at eleven." I glanced over my shoulder at the clock behind me. Eight-thirty. I had plenty of time. "I'm going to need a serious caffeine hit for today." I started to sit up, but Brandon's hand grabbed mind.

"Where are you going?"

"To put on makeup. I must be rather frightening after staying up so late."

He tugged me back down and ran his fingers down my face. "I've told you a million times you don't need makeup, and I've always meant it. You're beautiful with or without it. Besides, you have plenty of time to get dressed for the brunch." His fingers entwined with mine. "Relax. I only want to spend some time with you before I have to share you with everyone else."

The gold flecks in his hazel eyes popped in the sun peeking in through the curtains, his cheeks held more stubble than yesterday from the overnight growth, and his lips almost appeared soft for a man's. All I knew is one moment I studied his precious face and the next, my lips were pressed to his, completely forgetting this was Brandon. Brandon, the boy I played Super Mario Bros. with as a child, Brandon, the one who beat up Casey Fontaine when he grabbed my ass junior year, and Brandon, the one who enjoyed tormenting me more than anyone I knew.

I'd been the one to reach across that divide and initiate whatever it was I was doing, startling him by the jump when my lips met his. He froze for a moment, his hand stiff in mine, but when I began to draw back, his lips claimed mine by teasing the bottom and the top with a groan that made me rub my thighs together. How did he do that without touching me?

His hand released mine to wrap around me and pull me closer while he continued to tease my lips with soft kisses that messed with my ability to put together any sort of coherent thought. Once I was pressed flush to his body, his fingers wove through my hair, gripping it as his kiss became more demanding. His tongue dipped in to caress mine and I dug my fingers into his sides in an attempt to ground myself somehow. His free hand cupped my rear and drew my hips to his.

He felt so good, so strong, and I didn't want whatever this was to end. Brandon's body couldn't be pressed close enough, and his hand stroking along my skin, slipping under my tank top and stroking the underside of my breast made me dizzy. I'd never felt like this—never been this turned on in my life. If only he'd touch that spot, the one now aching with need, I'd shatter faster than glass breaking against a granite countertop.

My hands grasped his rear and pulled him against me, giving my own groan when his hardness rubbed just the right spot. His lips latched onto my neck as I arched my back and held on for dear life.

Knock, knock, knock! "Jena, you little whore! You'd better be in there or I'm going to have kittens!"

Brandon slumped on top of me as the moment died a quick and painful death. "Charlie, I'm going to kill you," he muttered. He pushed himself up from me. "You didn't leave Charlie a note, did you?"

"It was dark. I didn't want to wake her up."

"Jena!" called Charlie from the other side of the door.

Without much effort, he lifted himself from the bed, grabbing a pillow to cover the impressive tent in his shorts. "Hold your horses! Did you consider that a phone might be a better option than waking the entire resort!"

Before he could open the door, I jumped from the bed and straightened the covers. The last thing I wanted was to give Charlie any ideas about what her brother and I were doing—for a myriad of reasons!

The door swung open and Charlie didn't wait for an invitation. She stomped forward into the room, her index finger outstretched and pointing at me while Brandon headed for the bathroom. "Don't do that again! I don't care if you want to sleep somewhere else, but wake me the fuck up first. Got it?"

I crossed my arms tightly over my chest. "I'm sorry."

"You should be." Her hands landed on her hips and everything about the way she stood screamed attitude. "You have no idea how worried I was when I woke up and all your crap was gone. For all I knew, you'd spent the night on the beach." She spun around on her heel, her messy bun flapping with the abrupt movement. "I'll see you at brunch. Maybe I'll have cooled off by then." She started through the door but glanced back at me over her shoulder. "But maybe not."

I closed the door behind her and rubbed my face with my hands. "You could've texted her on your way down. Charlie has a short fuse, but I'd be worried as hell too."

I blew out a long breath and turned to where he stood in the bathroom doorway. "I know. I should've let her know. It's no excuse, but I was so tired I couldn't see straight. I honestly never thought about it."

He scratched the back of his head. Did the room suddenly shrink? It closed in a little more, and the air became thick and difficult to draw into my lungs. His hand dropped with a thud to his side. "Why don't I order some coffee and a light breakfast while you take a shower?"

I nodded but stood rooted to my spot. Why couldn't I move? My palm rubbed across my stomach as I looked up to find him taking four determined strides to stand almost toe to toe with me.

"What's wrong?" He cradled my chin in his palms, ensuring I held his eye.

"I didn't plan to kiss you. I think now I'm trying to figure out whether I should've."

"Why did you do it then?"

"Because I wanted to. Please don't think I didn't. It was this crazy impulse, and for the first time in a long time, I didn't think before I acted."

"That's not a bad thing, you know." He raked his fingers through my hair but kept one hand on my cheek. "You always overanalyze and overthink everything. Maybe you let your heart overrule your head for once?"

"I hadn't thought about it that way."

He tugged me closer and kissed my forehead. "I'm not sorry you did it. I've dreamed of kissing you and holding you like this for so long."

My heart rate began to pick up speed and thudded loudly in my ears. Could I let go of the worries and doubts that plagued my thoughts and just let myself be with Brandon? What if I couldn't, and I hurt him in the process?

"Stop it, Jena." He tipped my chin up. "I can feel you tensing, and I can tell your brain is starting to whir with a million questions. Don't do that to yourself. Just live in the moment with me because I want to do the same with you."

"What if we hurt one another?" My voice wavered and cracked. I wouldn't cry!

"Whether we're successful or not, we might hurt one another. Every couple has arguments that wound. We have no promise that it will work, but I know a relationship between us will. You're the only woman I want to wake up every morning with—even if you're not wearing makeup. I'm not leaving or running away. We can go as slowly as you want."

I gnawed at my lip while I stared at that small notch at the base of his throat. Was Brandon whom I was meant to be with all along? Could everything be that simple? I snapped out of my thoughts when he pulled my lip from my teeth.

"You don't have to make your mind up this minute," he said. "Just let me take you out on a date."

"How would that be different from what we normally do?"

With a shrug, he took my hands, rubbing his thumbs over the tops. "More handholding, something romantic . . . I don't know . . . at least a kiss goodnight." A mischievous grin lit his face when he brought up the kiss, making him look a lot like he did when he was a boy. "I'd love to dance with you tonight."

"I might be able to arrange that." My voice was all breathy and weird. Good grief! Was I as bad as Misty, the front desk hussy?

He wrapped his arms around me and drew me into a hug as he pressed a kiss to my forehead. "Go jump in the shower and I'll get that light breakfast ordered. We can take our time getting ready."

"Okay," I said in almost a whisper.

One problem with Brandon's confession was that it made me self-conscious while we got ready. I showered, and even though I wore one of the resort's robes, I still felt naked. When he disappeared into the bathroom for his shower, I rushed to get dressed. Our breakfast arrived right before he stepped back into the room, his black boxer briefs clinging to places I'd never thought to look before. My face never stopped burning while I put on my makeup, which made matters difficult, to say the least!

Later, when I arrived in the small dining room set aside for the brunch, I was the first to show until a few minutes later when my sister walked in. Ellie lifted her eyebrows when she noticed me. "You might want to steer clear of Charlie. She's still spitting fire over your disappearance last night."

"I apologized," I said with a sigh. "I was so tired and couldn't sleep with her snoring. I was desperate for a few hours, so I hurried out in the middle of the night. I probably would've slept longer this morning if she hadn't started banging on the door like she did." Hardly! But Ellie didn't need to know what would've kept me awake.

"She was really worried."

"I know. I'm sorry."

She lifted that one eyebrow that during certain conversations could make me squirm. "I assume you went to Brandon's room."

"I had nowhere else to go."

Ellie wore a small smile on her lips. "Something's going on between the two of you. You've been acting strange, he was hardly around for the last week or so, and a moment ago, he walked you to the door of the dining room. He kissed the back of your hand, Jena."

My cheeks heated, and I stared at my rose-colored pumps as Ellie's eyes bored into the side of my head. Would I ever stop blushing? "We're going to try dating." The clink of glass on the table drew my eyes. Ellie grasped my upper arms, her eyes bulging from their sockets.

"Are you serious?" She started bobbing up and down on her toes. "Don't lie to me. I won't tell anyone if you want to keep it quiet, but tell me the truth."

"We argued yesterday because I've been avoiding him. He told me he's been in love with me for a long time, which made me feel even more awkward."

"That's why you wanted to stay with me or Charlie."

"Yes," I said. "But I had to give in. We talked about it this morning and agreed to try dating." I hugged my arms around myself. "I'm still not sure. What if we ruin our friendship?"

"You won't." Ellie's tone rang of her certainty. "The two of you are perfect for each other. As long as the chemistry is there, you don't have anything to worry about." Her head tilted down a fraction. "The chemistry is there, isn't it?"

I nodded and clasped my hands together awkwardly in front of me. "Oh, yeah. I never paid attention to him that way in the past, but this morning, the sight of him in those boxer briefs . . ."

A girlish giggle burst from her, reminding me of nights we talked about boys while polishing off pints of ice cream. "Good! It's about time you lusted after a man."

"I've—"

"Don't even try to defend yourself. I think you've liked the men you've dated, but how often did you truly want to sleep with one? Connor was the first in what, two or three years? Even then, you confided the night after you broke up with him that he'd been mediocre in bed." I opened my mouth to speak, but she held up a hand. "Don't deny it. You may have been drinking, but you did use the word 'mediocre.' Why would you want to spend your life with so-so?"

William's sister, Addy, walked in and glanced between us. "I'm not interrupting, am I?"

"No," I said before clearing my throat. "We were just chatting."

"I passed Charlie's brother on my way. That's one good looking man."

I'm sure my mouth dropped open. "Addy?"

The younger woman rolled her eyes. "Sheesh! I'm married, not dead. What I want to know is how you've resisted that for so long. You've been friends with him for how many years?"

Ellie took Addy by the arm. "I've already been pestering her. Let's leave the poor thing alone."

"Leave what poor thing alone?" said Charlie as she walked into the private dining room.

"No one," I replied without giving time for a muscle to twitch.

"PMS much?" Charlie shoved her hands in the pockets of her dress pants. Why did she get to wear such casual clothing? Ellie said dresses.

"All right." My sister's peacemaking voice emerged. "This is my wedding day, remember? Now, I'm starving for the first time in two months. Let's eat."

Charlie stepped beside me as I followed Ellie. "I'm still mad at you."

"I'm sorry."

"I know, but I'm not ready to forgive you yet."

Chapter 7

While I waited near the table reserved for the wedding party, Ellie and William greeted guests near the entrance of the open air tent the resort erected for the reception. The ceremony had been small and intimate with only close friends and family on the beach to witness the happy couple's heartfelt vows. Now, they were joined by more of their friends and a few business associates for the celebration.

Micah, a friend of Ellie's, buzzed around taking photos of everything. He was our go-to guy for weddings even though he could photograph anything and make it look amazing. He'd taken stunning maternity portraits of Ellie when she was pregnant with Freya, and he took all of the photos of us and the office for our company website.

A bout of giggling drew my eyes to a tiny, little girl sneaking between the skirts of two ladies. She headed toward the entry, but before she could get far, I scooped her up from behind and tickled her side. "What are you up to, Freya?"

"I want Daddy," she said, pointing toward William.

"He's greeting guests right now. Why don't we watch from here, and as soon as he's done, I'll take you to him?" She frowned at me, but I poked her in the tummy, making her break a smile while she grabbed where I'd poked.

"Thank goodness you caught her." Addy squeezed between two guests, straightening her blue bridesmaid gown once she'd made it through. "One moment, she was at my feet and the next she was gone."

I tugged at the front of Freya's frilly flower girl dress. "You know better than to run off. Weren't you supposed to hold Aunt Addy's hand?" Freya nodded, but her sad eyes and serious face didn't fool me. I hoisted her up a bit higher on my hip while ensuring the skirt of my dress didn't come with her. "You need to tell her you're sorry."

Freya's shoulders lifted while she tilted her head. "Sowwy, Aunt Addy."

Addy sighed and sagged against the back of the nearest chair. "Is it awful that I can't stay mad at her? What are Ben and I going to do for an entire week? She's going to bat her eyelashes and get whatever she wants."

I couldn't help but smile. "It's tempting, but you're going to have to put your foot down. She's so much like Ellie was as at this age. By the stories my dad tells, Ellie got into everything. He hated it, but he had to be the bad guy."

"Your mom wouldn't discipline the two of you?"

At the mention of my mother, I sucked some air between my teeth. "My mother was more likely to rant and exclaim that she washed her hands of Ellie. Dad was better off handling any problems Ellie had. No matter what I did, Mom always claimed I was perfect. Poor Dad couldn't win and had to be the disciplinarian for both of us."

"I apologize for asking, but I always felt awkward asking your sister. It's just that your mother is never around."

"No. Ellie got tired of always being wrong and the problem child. Over time, she's slowly separated herself from our mother. It was the right decision for her."

Addy watched Ellie and William. "But you must have a very different relationship with your mother?"

"I did at one time. My mother has been very critical of me opening a business with Ellie and Charlie. She also favored one man I dated and became angry when the relationship ended.

She's insistent that if I don't marry in the next few years, I'll grow old and die all alone. Since then, I call her on holidays, but I've had to give her some space. She moved to Atlanta a few months ago to be closer to her sister. That's helped a lot."

"Here's your wine."

I startled a bit when Brandon held the bowl-shaped glass of red wine in front of me. "Here, let me take her." He placed both glasses on the table behind me and took Freya into his arms, tapping his index finger to her nose. "What are you getting up to, Miss Freya?"

"She ran away from Addy and was heading in William's direction."

Freya pointed toward William. "I want Mommy and Daddy."

Behind us, the band started playing, and Brandon gave an excited gasp. "Why don't we dance?"

He stepped out of the tent and onto a patch of grass where he could have more room, took Freya's hand, and started to sway back and forth.

A whoosh of breath came from Addy. "God, if that was Ben, we'd be disappearing to our room as soon as William and Ellie were free. That's sexy as hell, not to mention enough to ramp up my baby-making hormones."

I picked up my glass of wine and took a sip, clenching my free hand since I was tempted to fan myself with it. I'd seen Brandon hold Freya before, I'd seen him talk to her, and I'd seen him read her a book when I was babysitting her. I'd always found it adorable, but at those times, it didn't make me want to throw him down and do dirty things to him. Now, I envisioned very dirty things. Yes, my mind had gone there and wasn't considering returning for some time.

A laugh came from beside me. "You might want to wipe your chin."

I glanced over at Addy and gave a joking sneer. "Shut up."

"And here I thought the two of you were nothing more than friends." She said it in that annoying sing-song voice that made me want to deny everything—not that I had much to tell. "I will say that I don't know why you've waited for so long. He's hot."

"It's not . . ." What was I supposed to say? We'd agreed to go on a few dates, but what was that? We hadn't even started yet, so I couldn't really say we were dating.

"Oh!" Addy's eyes widened. "You're only now realizing you are attracted to him. I remember that."

"You?"

"Ellie never told you?" She took a glass of champagne from a passing tray, took a sip, and held it while she crossed her arms. "Ben and I first met when I was twelve. We both attended an orchestra camp at Furman University and became friends. After that, we attended almost all of the same music camps and events until we graduated high school. We planned on attending Boston Conservatory together, but I never thought of it as more than friendship until then."

Brandon grinned at me, making my stomach do a full-on somersault while Freya chattered on about some nonsense. "How did you know he was the one?"

Addy looped her arm through mine and leaned against me like the secret of the universe was on the tip of her tongue.

"Because I was more terrified of living my life without him than I was being in a relationship with him."

I blinked and turned to face her. "But that doesn't make sense. What if you'd given it a shot, but you lost him because the relationship failed?"

She took both my hands and squeezed. "That man is in love with you. If you continue on as you have, he'll eventually find it's too painful to remain friends, and your friendship will end. Do you want that? He can only swallow his heart so many times. Whether you try or not, you risk losing him."

My eyes burned and I blinked. I wouldn't cry. Ellie would be furious if I showed up for pictures with red, bloodshot eyes from crying.

"I'm sorry," said Addy quietly. "I don't mean to upset you. I know it's hard. I had a difficult time coming to terms with the change in my relationship with Ben, and we didn't even have your history. We were more pen pals for most of the year rather than every day playmates."

"What's going on?" I cleared my throat and plastered a smile on my face when I pivoted back to face Brandon, who walked toward us, hand in hand with Freya.

"Just talking." I blinked and took a large sip of my wine to cover my silliness.

"It looks like Ellie and William are done greeting guests. We should probably head over for pictures before the party gets swinging," said Addy as she held out her hand. "Come on, Freya. Let's go see your daddy." At the word daddy, Freya's face lit, and she rushed forward to go with Addy while I lagged behind with Brandon.

"You looked upset for a moment." After I set my glass on the table, his hand trailed down the inside of my bare arm until his fingers laced with mine.

"I'm fine. I promise." I nudged his bicep with my shoulder. "I enjoyed watching you with my niece. Quite sexy, Dr. Taylor."

His face reddened as he grinned. "You liked that, did you? Maybe I should change jobs and babysit? You could come along and watch."

"Or maybe we should try a puppy or a kitten and see if it gets the same reaction?" Was I actually flirting? Well, I suppose it was all or nothing! Addy's words made sense. I couldn't expect him to stay in a platonic relationship forever when he desired more. I needed to ignore the fears holding me back. If only I could figure out how.

"Mr. Middleton is bringing in his Springer puppies next week to have their dew claws removed. I might be able to arrange something."

"Will you two stop making eyes at each other and get your fine asses over here." Micah stood about five feet away, at the edge of the tent, one hand on his hip and a foot thrown out in true runway model fashion. "Come on, lovebirds. We don't have all night."

"Does he speak like that at every wedding he photographs?" asked Brandon.

"No, he's usually very professional, but he's more a guest than he is working tonight. His gift to Ellie is the pictures. Besides, it's not like the entire tent could hear. Most of the guests have found people they know who are already inside or they're milling around the bar." The bar was situated on the opposite end of the tent. With the music, Micah's voice wouldn't have been noticed.

When we reached the latticework trellis laden with bougainvillea, Micah arranged us and proceeded to click away with his camera. The pictures with the bridesmaids and groomsmen didn't take long, so after the last shot, Brandon tilted his head toward the tent. "Do you need to wait for Freya?"

"No, Addy is remaining behind. See?" I pointed to William's sister, who stood off to the side. "Since she lives in Boston, she doesn't spend so much time with Freya. She and her husband are going to stay in William and Ellie's house with her for the next few days. Then William and Ellie will take Freya with them for the rest of their honeymoon."

"Do you know where they're going?" he asked as I looped my arm through his and we started back toward the tent.

"They're taking Freya to Disney World."

His forehead wrinkled, and his eyebrows drew together. "Isn't she a little young?"

"For some of the attractions, but they have rides for little ones and other things to do. Ellie doesn't like roller coasters or even Ferris wheels, and because she's pregnant, she shouldn't be riding some of the more daring rides. It's more about them spending time together."

"I can appreciate that," he said, pulling me a bit closer. "Have I told you that you look stunning in that particular shade of blue?"

"Thank you." I glanced down at my dress. Ellie let us each pick our own with the stipulation that we all had to wear a shade of blue. Luckily, Emma coordinated a great selection that looked beautiful together but gave us each the choice of an individual look we might enjoy wearing again. Mine was slate blue with thin straps and an empire waist that gradually flared into a flowy, gauzy skirt.

"Hey." He bumped me with his elbow. "Will you dance with me tonight?"

When I glanced up, his eyes caught mine and held. "Yes," I replied simply, trying to keep from shaking. Why was I this nervous about a dance? I'd danced with Brandon before, so it wasn't like this would be the first time.

When we stepped back into the reception, my father stood near the door with Melanie. "There you are. How much longer before the happy couple returns?"

"Micah is finishing up the pictures of just the two of them and a few with Freya," I said. "They should be back soon."

My father held out his hand. "Brandon, it's good to see you." When Brandon took his hand, my father put his other arm around Melanie. "I'd like you to meet Melanie. Melanie, when these two were growing up, this boy practically lived at my house, and if he wasn't there, I always knew Jena could be found at his house. The two of them were very predictable."

Brandon smiled and shook Melanie's hand. "It's good to see you, Ms. King. How's Jethro?"

She giggled while she hip-bumped my father. "He's fine. Probably sleeping on his favorite memory foam bed at my neighbors' home. I'm sure you know the Daleys."

"Oh, yes. They lost their Golden Retriever last year. How are they?"

"They're good. At their age, they decided not to get another dog, so they take care of Jethro when I'm at work or at school. He loves going to their house for the day."

With a nod, Brandon shoved his free hand into his pocket. "That's wonderful. They can still enjoy having a pet without the worry of finding someone to care for it if one of them becomes ill. They also don't have the stress of paying for treatment. We helped them out as much as we could when their dog began to decline."

"Exactly," said Melanie. "And they've spoken so highly of you and your father. They appreciated everything you did. The current situation works out well for everyone, and Jethro is definitely happy not to be alone all day long."

My dad's shoulders shook a bit from chuckling. "I forgot you know Brandon because of your dog."

Melanie rolled her eyes. "Well, the Taylors *are* the best vets in town."

When I glanced up, Brandon's cheeks had reddened again. I'd always found it endearing that he blushed when someone praised him. I bumped my shoulder into his side, and he shrugged. "Thank you. My father and I appreciate your kind words."

Dad chuckled and held up his beer. "I'm sure the two of you have something more fun to do than talk to us."

"Dad," I said, chiding him. He loved to make statements that weren't necessarily true but were more for a reaction.

"Brandon, go get my daughter a glass of wine. She still looks rather uptight."

Brandon didn't laugh out loud, but he did give a slight shake to his head while his shoulders shook. He knew my father well, so the statement clearly wasn't shocking to him. "Yes, sir." He looked to Melanie and gave a quick dip of his chin. "It's good to see you, Ms. King."

Melanie waved to Brandon, but when he turned to lead me away, she winked at me, making me almost trip on my dress. How did my dad find a woman nearly as candid as he was?

"Another Malbec?"

I followed as he tugged me away. "Yes, please."

"I think Ms. King is good for your father. He seems happier than he's been in the past, and their personalities work well together. They're both outspoken, intelligent, and enjoy teasing."

"I think so too." After he placed the drink order with the bartender, his hand dropped down to mine and pulled me closer. "What kind of dog is Jethro?" I asked.

"He's a beagle. She adopted him from a rescue a few years back. He'd been part of a litter that had been dumped on the side of the road. I suppose they couldn't sell them, or they weren't going to make the money they thought they would. Too many people breed their dogs without realizing the expense and can't make their money back. When they finally understand how much it's going to cost them, they dump them."

When the bartender set down my wine, I took a sip. "I know you miss having a pet since you moved out of your parents' house. It's been two years. I've wondered for some time why you haven't adopted one yet." Brandon had always been very vocal on adopting pets from the shelter or rescues.

He would never buy one from a breeder when so many pets didn't have forever homes.

He watched our hands while he laced his fingers with mine. "I was waiting for you. I know it probably sounds ridiculous, but I want us to have a pet together. Not for me to have one you tolerate. I thought we'd pick out a puppy and a kitten, so they'd be raised together. You've always preferred cats."

I smiled that he remembered. "I have."

Before I could say more, everyone clapped as Ellie and William re-entered the reception. I wish we could've talked more then and there, but we found ourselves surrounded by other guests during dinner. People crowded around while the happy couple cut the cake and drank sparkling cider. Soon, the time came when Brandon had to go stand with the rest of the eligible bachelors while William threw Ellie's garter.

One side of Brandon's lips lifted when he peered over at me. Of course, William took that moment to shoot the garter right into Brandon's chest. He turned a vivid shade of crimson but was a good sport, laughing and spinning the crocheted elastic band around his finger.

"All right, all you single ladies!" I groaned when the DJ started playing Beyoncé's song while Ellie danced and waved the bouquet in the air.

Brandon held out his hand but yanked me forward. "Come on! It's your turn!"

My father stood across from the group of women in the center, clapping, and by the grin on his face, thoroughly enjoying the spectacle as Melanie joined me and Charlotte.

My sister turned her back to us, dropped her arm, and tossed the cluster of flowers over her head. I started to step back, but a hand to each of my arms steered me directly into the path of the oncoming bouquet and an "umph" came from my side. As the flowers landed in my arms, a woman fell to the floor. Charlotte stood at that shoulder with one hand on my upper arm and a completely wide-eyed, innocent expression on her face. The little witch pushed someone out of the way, so I would catch it! This was no coincidence but a coordinated attack. When my head whipped around to Melanie, she leaned closer. "Now, go dance with that boy. You know you want to."

Ellie hugged us both before she joined William and Freya on the dance floor. The three of them exuded this joy and peace I longed to have, but was Brandon the one to give that to me?

"Dance with me?"

His breath made goosebumps pebble the skin under my ear and the deep, melting chocolate tone of his voice caused my stomach to flip. Even if he hadn't held my hand, the tone of his request was enough to drag me behind him onto the dance floor like a pathetic puppy dog on an invisible leash. My heart picked up its pace as he wrapped his arms around me and began moving.

The song possessed a slow, sensuous beat and our bodies brushed each other as he swayed me to the music. The strong muscles of his shoulder and back shifted under my palm, his lips caressed my temple, creating a spark that traveled everywhere, and the hand against my lower back pressed me closer, until no more space existed between us—so little space that he couldn't have hidden that he was just as aroused as I was if he'd tried.

"Take a walk on the beach with me."

After I nodded, he led me through the side of the covered reception area directly into the sand. My heels sank, and I pulled back on his arm. "Wait, I need to take off my shoes."

I didn't bother unbuckling the straps but slipped them off and set them against a column. I didn't want to have to carry them with me.

Brandon's steps were unhurried. We meandered to the waters' edge while the music filtered along the breeze, adding an intimate current to the moment. After we strolled the curve that followed the waterline, most of the light from the resort had faded.

The next thing I knew, Brandon held me tightly in his arms, and his lips claimed mine in a kiss that was neither gentle nor soft. Instead, it spoke of hunger and need as he tugged greedily at my lips and tasted me with his tongue. My knees wobbled, but I wrapped my arms tightly around his neck, whole-heartedly giving back what he doled out. His fingers dug into my hair and held me to him while his free hand clenched my skirt, bunching it so it was snug around my waist.

I still don't know how he ended up sitting on the sand with me straddling his waist, but as his hand slid up my thigh to my rear and gripped the flesh, a high laugh from somewhere in the distance jolted me from the fog in my brain.

"Brandon," I said, my voice hoarse. "Anyone could see us here."

He released the spot he'd been suckling at the base of my neck and rested his head against my shoulder. "Is it bad that I don't care?" He rubbed his hand up and down the underside of my thigh. "God, you feel amazing. Your skin is so soft."

I gently kissed his lips, caressing his cheeks with my fingertips. The dim light still allowed me to see his eyes. I couldn't look away. Was I terrified of this? Undoubtedly, but I couldn't live without him. That simple truth seeped into my skin and filtered into my bones without any huge fanfare or spectacle. The thought of us not at least being friends terrified me. I always felt myself when I was with him, and right now, my body hummed with want and need and every other messy urge I couldn't name. I'd never been this turned on in my life. So, I did the only thing I could do. I held on to his steady gaze. "I want you."

Chapter 8

His eyes flared and his hand clenched my thigh. "Jen, I thought you wanted to go slow."

"I know. Chalk it up to a woman's prerogative to change her mind."

His forehead dropped to my chest as his back expanded with the heavy breath he drew into his lungs. "I can't lie. Just your saying that made me so hard, I don't know if I can walk, much less think with my brain and not my dick."

"You're so romantic," I said, laughing.

"I'm sorry. I've wanted you for so long. You don't know how badly I'm fighting this caveman urge to beat my chest, throw you over my shoulder, and take you back to my room."

I laid my cheek on the top of his head. "The grunting might be sexy." His warm chuckle made me smile and kiss the tip of his ear.

His head shifted as his lips caressed my collar bone, then my neck, and finally my lips. "I don't want you to regret something done on impulse." His eyes held mine while his fingers trailed down my leg.

"A person can have regrets whether something is spur of the moment or it's thought out for months or even years," I said softly. "Neither of us can predict what will happen, but I'm ready to say fuck it."

He grinned at my uncharacteristic swear. "Fuck it, huh?" After one more lingering kiss, his hand took mine. "I want to dance with you at least one more time. Why don't we return to the party, and we'll take the rest of the evening as it comes?" I opened my mouth, but he put his finger over my lips. "I'm not saying you don't know your own mind. I swear. I'm just not sure about a mad dash for the room. Besides, we can't get back there without passing in front of the reception. What if we run into Charlie . . . or your dad."

I scrunched my nose. "Oh, that would be awkward."

He pressed me back to stand and rose. "The thought got rid of my hard-on but quick." He brushed the sand from his pants and took my hand as we headed back toward the open-air tent, stopping briefly to pick up my shoes. "Do you want another glass of wine?"

"No." I shifted closer until I was flush to his arm and leaned my head on his shoulder. "Two is plenty."

When we approached the tent, a slow ballad filtered out into the darkness, and I stopped, tugging Brandon back. "Dance with me here." We still stood outside of the light from the party. With the potted plants arranged around the periphery of the reception, we retained a certain amount of privacy.

"Here? In the sand?"

I nodded. "In the twilight, under the stars. Just us."

He drew me into his arms while I wrapped mine around his shoulders. My feet inched between his as he began swaying to the melody. I didn't lay my head on his shoulder or on his chest. Instead, I tucked it into that crook between his chin and his shoulder, pressing my lips to the sensitive flesh. His hands slid from my waist to my lower back, which I took as permission to continue, so I lightly nipped at the base of his neck.

He inhaled sharply as his fingers dug into my back, clenching my dress. "Jena," he half-groaned, half-whispered. "You're making this impossible."

I suckled the same spot as his breathing became quicker. When I lifted my head, my teeth had barely grazed his earlobe as he turned, so his lips captured mine. His palms cradled my rear and pushed my hips forward to meet his, his erection pressing insistently against the top of my thigh. I gasped when he moved to my neck and mimicked what I'd done to him a few moments before.

"Come." To my own ears, my voice sounded odd—low and a bit hoarse as if I couldn't catch my breath.

I took his hand and drew him along behind me. We crept to one side of the tent, keeping out of the light until we walked behind the bougainvillea trellis that hid us from everyone. Brandon scanned his key card on the pad near the door. Our room was on the other side of the hotel, but if we passed through, we might avoid most of the people we knew.

We tiptoed through the hall, turned the corner, and halted when my dad and Melanie stood in front of me. Melanie pressed her lips together while my father's eyes wandered up and down Brandon and then me. I brushed my hand down the front of my dress. Nothing was out of place, was it? I tucked my hair behind my ear and stood straight. I'd been an adult for how long? It was time to act like one.

Dad cleared his throat. "Well, we were headed to bed. Enjoy the rest of your night." His one eyebrow lifted. Lord, I wanted to throw my skirt over my head and hide!

Brandon coughed. "You too, sir."

We moved to opposite sides of the hall and passed. Suddenly, our destination didn't seem so urgent as it had before. After we crossed the lobby, Brandon pulled me into his arms and gave me a quick kiss. "Meet me in the room. I'll be there in a minute."

"Where are you going?"

"You'll see." He winked at me and pushed me forward. "Go on. I won't be long."

I passed no one else between the lobby and our room, and after I closed the door behind me, I glanced around while blowing out a heavy exhale. We were going to do this? Yes, we were going to do this. Crap! We were going to do this!

I hurried to the bathroom and nearly fell over at the sight of myself in the mirror. Holy cow! No wonder Dad looked at me as though I'd sprouted a third head. My hair was falling from its pins, my lipstick was completely gone, and I tilted my head to the side to examine a hickey the size of a quarter at the base of my neck. That wouldn't be easy to cover on Monday morning.

Before I could second guess myself, I pulled the pins from my hair, letting it fall in layers past my shoulders. A quick sniff to my armpits passed muster. I wore new lace panties with a matching strapless bra, so I was good to go there.

I stared at myself for a moment or two before I removed my jewelry and unzipped my dress. Was I actually going to do this? I'd never been this ballsy in the past. I swallowed down the butterflies fluttering between my stomach and my chest. When the dress hung in the closet, I shook my hands, trying to alleviate some of my nervous energy as I scanned the room. What was I supposed to do? It wasn't like I'd ever tried to be seductive before.

I crawled onto the bed and laid on my stomach, my legs bent at the knees, and my feet in the air. I'd just planted my elbow and propped my head on my hand when Brandon walked in the door, giving me no time to second guess myself. He stumbled when he noticed me, barely saving himself from falling on his face before he backed against the door.

"Holy shit, Jena." He held a bottle of champagne in one hand and a clear plastic container in the other, though I couldn't see what was inside.

I pushed myself onto my knees and sat back. "Too much?"

"No . . . Yes . . . No." He nearly bludgeoned himself in the head with the bottle of champagne in an attempt to run a hand over his hair. "I swear. You're going to give me a heart attack." His eyes roved down my chest to my stomach and further, all the way down to the bed. I drew in a breath to calm that crazy squirming mass of nerves that might otherwise have kept me from following through. I stepped off the mattress and took what he held, placing it on the bedside table, and began to unbutton his shirt.

I pressed a kiss to that small hollow at the base of his neck while my fingers continued parting the fabric to expose his chest underneath. My lips then trailed up to his jaw as his head turned and his eyes latched onto mine. His strong hands landed on my hips, gripping for dear life.

With a groan, his lips found mine, brushing the top and then the bottom ever so slowly. I tugged his shirt from his pants and ran my palms up his washboard stomach, over the spattering of hair on his chest, to his shoulders, so I could push it down his arms. Hopefully, he wouldn't feel me trembling. I hadn't slept with many men, and I'd never taken the initiative. I'd never felt comfortable enough. A lack of confidence certainly wasn't hot.

"Cufflinks," he muttered against my mouth.

His arms wrapped around me, and after a small amount of fidgeting, he dropped them into his pocket. Gentle fingers trailed down my cheek, my neck, and the swell of my breast. "You're so freaking gorgeous."

He kissed me and whatever rational thought left in my head disappeared into the mist. His lips were firm, yet soft and cradled mine as his arms wrapped around me. I stepped back, and he followed until I stopped at the bed hitting the back of my legs. My bra fell from my chest and was swiftly tossed aside. I gasped as he lifted me and pressed me down into the mattress.

His weight on top of me wasn't heavy or oppressive but was oddly familiar and settled those butterflies I'd desperately wanted to banish from my stomach. Instead of that nervous quiver, my heart stuttered in my chest and I was warm—so very warm.

He pressed kisses down my body until he reached my breasts. His eyes locked with mine as he scraped his teeth along my nipple before taking it into his mouth and suckling. His gaze refused to release mine while he made my body act without thought. My breath started to quicken, my legs squeezed together in an attempt to alleviate that ache that hadn't gone away since our interlude on the beach, and my hands clenched the sheets, desperate to hold on to something solid. How did he do this to me with so little effort?

"Touch me," he whispered. His tongue trailed down to my belly button and back up to repeat what he'd done to the other side. I forced myself to release the sheet and reach for him, one hand massaging his shoulder while the other lightly scratched his back. His muscles tightened and relaxed under my palms. He felt so good, so strong, but I wanted more. My fingers threaded through his hair to drag him back to my lips.

I reached for his belt as our mouths tangled. I needed to feel all of him—as much as he could feel of me. His pants and his boxer briefs were shoved as far down as possible, so I could wrap my hand around his length.

"Oh, God," he groaned, covering my hand with his. "Jena, I won't last at this rate. I also only have one condom in my wallet. When I packed, I had no idea that we would do this. I'm not sure the one I have is even any good anymore."

"I'm on birth control and I'm healthy. We don't need a condom if you don't have one."

His chest heaved a shuddering breath. "I need it to keep from embarrassing myself. There's no way I'll last without it."

After a quick peck to my lips, he stood, removed his shoes, and pulled off his pants, removing his wallet from his pocket and throwing a packet on the bed. While he moved, I watched his muscles flex and release, and I admired his body. I'd never considered how toned and sexy he was until now. Why hadn't I? I had eyes—or had I been blind when it came to him and never paid attention?

He stood with his back to me, his shoulders heaving. I dragged myself to the end of the bed and stood on my knees, wrapping my arms around him from behind. "Are you okay?"

"I feel like a teenage boy who doesn't know what he's doing." His chest heaved and fell with his uneven breaths.

"In a way, I feel the same."

He chuckled and looked over his shoulder. "You feel like a teenage boy?"

I smiled, my lips against his skin. "No, this is so different—a good different. I don't want to do the wrong thing." My fingers traced his abs while I closed my eyes and leaned my forehead between his shoulder blades. I was dislodged when he turned.

"You haven't done anything wrong. You couldn't do anything wrong." He gently shoved me back onto the bed and removed my panties. My skin prickled as his eyes devoured me from my feet up to my face. He laid down on his stomach between my legs, and I shot up.

"You don't have to do that."

He rose enough to kiss me and press me back into the pillows. "Relax. I won't do anything you hate, but I've dreamed of tasting you, making you come this way."

"I've never let—" I gulped and dug my heels into the mattress. With him between my legs, I couldn't close them.

His lips grasped mine and he kissed me deeply. "Do you trust me?"

I stared into his eyes and nodded. I did trust him. I would trust him with my life.

My insides still clenched when he ran his hands down my body and shifted to my thighs. I was too nervous to watch him, so I closed my eyes.

At the first swipe of his tongue, I squirmed. It wasn't unpleasant, but it was a bit strange. When he focused on my clit, a noise I'd never heard before escaped from my throat. He drew that tiny piece of flesh into his mouth, and my back arched off the bed. I'd lost complete control over my own body, but despite my initial hesitancy, I never wanted him to stop. He pushed a finger inside, pressing up and rubbing on this one spot, and continued whatever he'd been doing before. An odd panting filled my head, my pulse pounded in my ears, and a radiating pressure began to build and spread until I begged and pleaded with him to continue. When all that pressure reached a breaking point, my eyes pressed shut as I shattered into a million pieces with a loud cry.

I couldn't move. I couldn't speak. Heck, I couldn't even open my eyes. The mattress dipped to either side of my shoulders and he kissed me. My hands grasped and pulled at the sheets while I kissed him back, as though I were dehydrated and he was the only source of water for miles.

The crinkling of the condom wrapper penetrated the sound of my heartbeat roaring in my ears. His weight pinned me down. "Jena, look at me." I dragged my impossibly heavy eyes open. "Are you sure?"

"Please," I whispered in a shaky voice.

That one word was all it took for him to fill me more than any man had in the past. After the orgasm, I wouldn't have expected to crest again, but as he thrust into me, he hit this spot that made me gasp and grab his ass to pull him in further. A low moan filled my ear as he held my hips and quickened his pace. "You're so tight. I love you. You have no idea how much." His words were disjointed, broken by his labored breathing and punctuated by his thrusts.

Before I could understand what was happening, my fingers dug into his backside, my thighs clenched his hips, and I saw stars as my head collapsed back. Sounds came from both of us, but my mind was overwhelmed by the pleasure I didn't know was possible. Nothing that was said made sense.

I'd barely opened my eyes when Brandon collapsed on top of me, his breathing making his shoulders and chest heave. Something wet tracked down my temple, and I lifted my hand to brush it away. Was I crying?

He lifted himself, and his relaxed face disappeared when he saw my face. "Are you okay? Did I hurt you?"

"No." I shook my head. "It was wonderful. I'm sorry." I choked back a sob. "I don't know why I'm crying. I feel so stupid."

He brushed my hair away from my face and caressed my lips with his. "Let me throw away the condom. I'll be right back. I promise."

I covered my face with my hands as he strode away. The water ran for a moment and the mattress sagged to one side when he returned. He tugged me against him, and I wrapped my arms around his chest and drew my leg onto his hip. His fingers grazed my back as he held me close.

His cologne mixed with his natural scent filled my nostrils. Somehow, a few deep breaths calmed and settled me. Why did it feel like I belonged nowhere but right here? I didn't want to overanalyze, so I lifted my head to the pillow where I could look at his face while we talked. "I'm sorry."

"For what?" His eyebrows dropped adorably in the middle.

"For being so silly. I'm overwhelmed, I guess. It's never been . . ." I sighed and concentrated on my fingers as they played with his chest hair. "It's not important." Maybe it was dark enough to hide the fact that my face, my neck, and my chest burned.

"Jena?" He lifted my chin. "Have you never had an orgasm before?"

Shit! He'd known me longer than anyone. I should've known I couldn't get away from this. "I've read enough magazines to know not all women have them during sex. I merely thought I was one of them. I've given them to myself but never had one with someone else."

He grabbed my hand and held it between us. "You haven't been with many men. What am I—the fourth? Most guys, when they're young, only care about themselves. As they get older, either they grow up or they're lazy and don't bother to change. Neither situation is your fault."

"Maybe," I said. Maybe the blame did lie with me on some level, but I didn't want to think about that yet. "What did you bring with the champagne?" It was fortunate I had an easy way to change the subject.

A huge grin lit his face as he rolled to his back and leaned against the headboard. He set the container in his lap and opened the flaps. "I believe these are your favorite. I'd noticed them on the dessert bar last night, so I checked with the kitchen to see if I could scrounge up a few."

Holding the sheet over my breasts, I lifted onto my elbow. Inside the box, were three huge, perfect, dark chocolate covered strawberries.

He set the strawberries back on the table, took one from the container, and yanked the sheet from my chest. "I'd originally gotten these as a romantic date thing to do. Now, I have more fun ideas in mind."

"Brandon," I said with a warning in my tone.

The strawberry pressed against my lips, the smell making my mouth water, and I sank my teeth into the crisp chocolate shell. The chocolate broke apart as the sweetness of the strawberry and the richness of the chocolate mingled on my tongue. I jumped and almost dribbled the treat from my mouth when the cold damp of the fruit landed on my neck and trailed down my chest.

"You're going to make a mess." The food in my mouth made it difficult to speak.

With his tongue, he followed the berry from under my chin to my nipple. He lightly bit and sucked before he took a bite of the strawberry and kissed me. "Sweet."

I giggled and reached to take another strawberry from the box. "We'll both need a shower when we're done."

As I pushed him down to the bed and crawled over him, his heady gaze wandered up and down my body and his voice turned heavy. "You'll get no complaints from me."

Chapter 9

Bright light seeped through my eyelids and woke me. I put out my hand to shield my eyes, but the slit in the heavy curtains provided the perfect angle, so the morning sun wouldn't leave me alone. Brandon's arm tightened around my stomach as his steady, even breathing blew in puffs along my neck. The clock's vivid red display read eight-fifteen. I let out a breath. I wasn't going to be able to sleep any longer.

Carefully, I unwound myself from Brandon's hold and nestled a spare pillow under his arm as a replacement. His dress shirt lay on the end of the bed, so I grabbed it and slipped it on.

My first stop was the bathroom. After the wine at the reception and the champagne we drank late last night, I couldn't avoid that one if I tried. Brandon's room boasted of a seriously nice bathroom too. The jacuzzi tub and enormous shower drew me in that direction, but I couldn't resist checking my reflection in the mirror.

My fingers touched my hair and then my cheek. Who was the woman staring back at me? Seriously! If I hadn't known it was me, I wouldn't have recognized myself. My tangled hair stood out from my head like I'd stuck my finger in an electrical socket. My eye makeup from last night was mostly gone, though it was smeared some, giving me a slight case of raccoon eyes. I winced at the thought of Brandon seeing me that way—of anyone seeing me that way.

I peered out of the door. Brandon was still sleeping. Perhaps I could wash my face and put on a light layer of makeup before he woke up. He always claimed I didn't need it, but I felt naked without it.

Once my face was washed, I reached for my makeup bag, nearly jumping out of my skin when two strong arms wrapped around me from behind. "What are you doing?"

"I washed my face. My mascara and eyeliner were smeared. I looked a mess."

"No, you didn't. You're always beautiful." He shifted my hair aside and kissed the back of my neck. One side of his hip peeked from the side of the shirt, reflecting in the mirror. He hadn't put on any clothes when he'd awakened.

A chuckle burst from my chest. "I'm beginning to think you're blind."

One of his hands reached out and took the satchel from my hand. "No makeup. You're gorgeous without it."

I grabbed the bag and caught his eye in the mirror. "At least let me put moisturizer on."

He nodded but didn't move or let me go. Instead, he continued kissing and nibbling at the back of my neck while one hand snaked under the wide, open collar of his shirt and began toying with my nipple. I never managed to remove the lid from the moisturizer jar since my hands clung to the counter, keeping me from falling to the floor in a heap.

"This isn't fair." My voice came out all raspy and low.

The opposite hand released my hair and wound around, finding its way through the opening in the lower portion of the shirt. His fingers slipped between my legs and I groaned and fell back against him. My head lolled against his shoulder as his teeth grazed along the sensitive skin under my ear. "Why is that?"

I couldn't stop staring in the mirror at the hand that parted the shirt tail and stroked up and down. To be fair, I'd made it ridiculously easy for him. Only two buttons held the article of clothing together while also leaving a large gap at the top and another at the bottom where he now gained access.

"I can't think when you do that," I said. One side of his lips curved up mischievously. "I have no control over my own body."

"I love that I can do that to you. You're always in such control of everything. You never let go. Do you have any idea how much of a turn on it is watching you lose yourself?" He pulled me back more into his erection. "Do you feel how much I want to be inside you right now?"

"Again?" One of his fingers dipped inside and a guttural noise trickled from my throat.

"Over and over and over. I'll never get tired of this."

Next thing I knew, I was bent forward toward the mirror as he slid home from behind. My hands grasped the counter until my knuckles were white, bracing myself against him as he began to thrust. Our gazes locked in the mirror and he snaked the arm under the bottom of his shirt to my shoulder to pull me back to him. I reached back with one hand to grasp his hip, desperate for him to fill me with every last precious inch.

I didn't need to worry since he pressed even deeper in that position. The slapping of our bodies filled the air. Every part of me prickled, sensitized in a way I couldn't describe if I tried, as that now familiar coiling wound through my body. I was going to burst. It was too intense.

"I can't. It's too much."

"Let go, Jena. I've got you."

I took a breath, but it stuttered to a halt as a strange incoherent cry rang from my lungs. My body froze. I couldn't move a muscle, yet Brandon kept dragging me back to meet him, the unbearable friction intensifying the waves of pleasure racking my body. When he growled my name, my fingernails dug into his hip, and I forced myself to continue his pace—to make his climax as intense as the one he'd just given me.

"Fuck, Jena." We tumbled back, landing with a thud on the mat. "I'm sorry. I couldn't hold myself up anymore." His arms held me tight against him as he buried his face into my neck.

I leaned my cheek against his damp hair. "We're going to need another shower."

He exhaled as his lips smiled against my shoulder. "Maybe we should actually use soap this time."

It hadn't been his fault we forgot soap. After the chocolate covered strawberries, we'd intended to shower, but I got carried away massaging his chest and let my hands wander downward. Two or three strokes made Brandon forget all about why we were under the hot spray of water in the first place.

"We can't take too long," I said. "We need to pack and check out."

His palm cradled my cheek and pulled my head around, so I could see his face. "Just in case I overslept, I booked the room for tonight as well." His eyes searched mine. "Stay with me? We can order room service and make love until we can't walk straight."

"Haven't we already achieved that noble ambition?"

"Probably, but I won't object to making it obvious to everyone who sees us." I shifted, so I could wrap my arm around his shoulders as he ran his thumb along my jawline. "I know we could go home and continue where we left off, but last night was amazing. I'm not ready to give that up yet."

"I don't have enough clothes."

"Perfect," he said, laughing. "Because we're not leaving this room. However, I won't object if you want to continue wearing that shirt. Once we're home, we'll need to have you try on my Clemson football jersey—but not during a game. I don't think I could pay attention to the field if you were wearing it."

"Do you need to go out for condoms?"

His forehead crinkled. "You said you're on birth control."

"Yes." I shrugged and watched our hands while I entwined my fingers with his. "But you still wore one the first time. I didn't know if you wanted the extra protection. I get a shot every three months, so it's not like I can forget a pill or anything. If you don't want to . . . "

He tipped my chin up with his finger. "I wasn't joking when I said I'd need it to last. Once I realized I was in love with you, no other woman held any interest for me."

My eyes stretched wide. "Surely you weren't completely celibate?"

"If you're asking if I manually took care of things, then no, I wasn't celibate. But that doesn't compare to a living, breathing interactive woman in bed—particularly when you've been in love with her for a few years. I needed the buffer, or I would've lost it the moment I was inside you—if I even made it that far."

"Well, you're certainly making up for lost time."

An incredulous bark burst from him before he rolled me to the floor and started tickling me mercilessly. "I haven't heard any objections, Miss Barrett. I seem to recall you begging more than once last night."

"Please, Brandon."

"Yup, you said that. I think you also said, 'Don't stop.'"

I couldn't stop laughing, but I couldn't fight back since he had my wrists pinned over my head with one hand while he straddled my waist. "You're cruel."

"No, you never said that. You definitely said 'faster.'"

"No more," I gasped. "Please."

The tickling stopped, and he bent forward and claimed my lips softly, sweetly as he released my hand. "I love you. I know you need time to figure out what's in your heart, and I'm more than willing to wait until you're ready to say those words. I hope you won't object to my saying them in the meantime. I've waited so long to tell you. I'm afraid I can't hold it back anymore."

"I don't mind. I do love you. I've loved you for as long as I can remember, but I need time to fall *in* love with you. You've had more time to come to terms with how you feel. I've only had a couple of crazy, confusing weeks." I glanced around me. "Not to interrupt the moment. I don't know about you, but I don't want to spend the rest of the day on the bathroom floor."

"No." He shook his head and pulled me up as he stood. "I was thinking about the jacuzzi tub, the bed, maybe the shower again." My eyes traced the stubble along his jaw down to his well-defined pecs and flat six-pack abs. As they ventured further, he lunged forward and grabbed me around the waist. "Before you start staring at me like you want to devour me whole, we need breakfast. I don't know about you, but I'm starving."

I slapped his chest and pushed him away. "I've never seen you naked before. I was simply looking."

"And your teeth scraped along your bottom lip like you were staring at a decadent piece of chocolate cake. You can look all you want—later, otherwise, we'll never eat."

"Breakfast, you mean?"

His eyebrows shot up, and I took off running into the bedroom, burying myself under the covers with only my head poking out as he strode into the room. One arm shot out and pointed at him. "Don't you dare tickle me again."

Instead of coming at me like I thought he would, he bent over and pulled on his boxer briefs. "Later. I told you I'm hungry." He rummaged around on the table and tossed the room service menu onto the bed. "What do you want?"

Carefully, I peeled away the sheet and comforter and rolled to my stomach, opening the menu. "It all looks amazing."

He crawled on top of me and lowered to his elbows so he looked over my shoulder. "Why don't we get several things and share? How about the pancakes, eggs benedict, and at least one side order of bacon?"

I blanched. "It's a good thing I exercise so much. I can't eat like this all of the time, you know."

"We burnt off enough calories last night to make up for it." He gave me a smacking kiss on the cheek, took the menu, and sat back on his heels while he dialed the extension printed on a card near the phone. "Yes, room 110 . . . We'd like an order of pancakes, eggs benedict, two sides of bacon, orange juice, coffee, and champagne . . . Thank you. Goodbye." When he hung up, he dropped the menu to the side of the bed. "It'll be twenty minutes." His hands ran up my back and his fingers began kneading at my shoulders.

"What do you want to do?" I was melting into the mattress by the second.

"I really don't want to cover you up, but we do have the patio with the table. Why don't we put on some clothes and eat outside, so we can enjoy the view? We can get our daily dose of vitamin D before I trap you indoors for the rest of the day."

"If you keep doing this, I won't ever move."

His husky laugh made me squeeze my legs together. How did he make me ache with something so simple? He stood and held out his hand to help me up. "The shirt stays on, just like this." He grabbed my jean cut-offs from the top of my suitcase. "You can put these on with it. I'll only be a few minutes." He went into the bathroom and shut the door behind him.

While he was gone, I put on the shorts and picked up the clothes on the floor. He came out while I was brushing the tangles from my hair. He stopped long enough to wrap an arm around me and kiss my neck but continued to pull on a pair of jeans and a t-shirt.

When I returned to the room, Brandon had opened the French doors. The room needed the fresh air. It'd been a bit musty and probably reeked of sex. After I pulled down the covers on the bed to air them as well, I walked outside and sat in one of the cushioned chairs. The waves lapped onto the sand before they receded back into the vast expanse of brilliant aquamarine water. The sound and the view relaxed every tight muscle in my body. I turned and leaned my head against the back of the chair for just a moment, basking in the warmth and the atmosphere.

"Jen." Soft lips brushed against my forehead. "Wake up, sleepyhead."

I blinked to find Brandon leaning over me, a smile adorning his face. "I fell asleep? For how long?"

"Not long. The food only just arrived." He tugged me up, sat in the chair, then situated me on his lap before pressing a flute of champagne into my hand. He held up his glass and tapped mine. "Thank you for staying another night with me."

"I have to. You're my ride." I held a serious expression for as long as I could before I snorted from trying to hold it in.

"That's hot," he said. He took a sip of his champagne and offered me a piece of bacon off the plate. "What time do you need to be at work tomorrow?"

"I don't have an appointment until the afternoon, so I'm in no hurry. However, I would like to get back before lunch to go over my accounts and schedule a few meetings."

"I have to be at the clinic for nine. If we're running late, you can always take my car and pick me up after work. We can go out to dinner."

"If we sleep as little as we did last night, I won't be good for much tomorrow evening."

"Then we can cuddle up on the sofa and watch a movie. I don't care what we do as long as I'm with you."

We did run late the next morning, so I pulled the SUV to the curb in front of the house and pulled my shoulders back. No doubt Charlie would have something to say. After all, the original plan consisted of coming home on Sunday night. I had a temporary reprieve from Ellie. She and William would be gone for the next two weeks honeymooning at Disney World. I just needed to survive Brandon's nosy and sometimes abrasive little sister.

The front door was already unlocked so I pulled my suitcase inside. Maggie, our receptionist, looked up when I walked in and rocked back in her chair, folding her arms over her chest. "Well, look at what the cat dragged in."

I pulled my hair around in a vain attempt to hide the evidence of what I'd been doing all weekend. "Sorry, I'm late. Traffic slowed us down."

She peered to the side to look out of the window. "Isn't that Brandon Taylor's car?"

"You know I went to the wedding with him. We decided to stay an extra night, and because we were delayed by traffic, I had to drop him off at work before I came here. Why am I explaining myself?"

Maggie shrugged with a giggle. "I don't know. Why do you feel the need?"

I started to walk forward but didn't quite get my foot in front of me when I noticed Charlie leaning against the door frame of her office. "An extra night, huh?"

I needed to play it cool. It wasn't any of Charlie's business—it wasn't anyone's business but mine and Brandon's. "Yup, it's a great resort." I grabbed the handle of my suitcase and began rolling it behind me toward the stairs, hoping to avoid an inquisition, but the little hussy followed me. Fortunately, she was on the opposite side of the obvious evidence.

"What exactly did the two of you do? Shuffleboard?"

Had lots of sex, ate room service, and had more sex in the jacuzzi. "Nothing exciting."

I picked up my bag and carried it upstairs while Charlie walked alongside me. "You must've had something special to do or you wouldn't have stayed. You could've done nothing exciting at home."

When I reached the top, I whirled on my heel and faced her head on. "What's the big deal? So, we stayed an extra night. I don't see why it's important." Her head tilted to the side as her eyes drifted to my now exposed neck. I winced. Crud! My hair had fallen down my back. I'd forgotten about the hickey.

"That's impressive. Did Brandon give you that when you were sucking face on the beach?"

"I'm not sure. You keep asking these questions. Do you truly want every sordid detail from this weekend?"

Charlie's shoulders dropped. "No, I don't, but I do want my brother happy. He's had feelings for you for a long time and this has seemed to bloom overnight. Don't hurt him or I'll kick your ass."

I involuntarily flinched. "I don't want to hurt him. This isn't exactly easy for me, you know."

She started back down the stairs but stopped a few steps down. "I never thought it was. For the record, I plan on giving him the same warning. He might be my brother, but you and Ellie are both like sisters to me. You're all my family. I don't want any of you hurt."

I nodded. "Got it."

I watched her return downstairs and glanced around the house. "Why does everything seem so different?" It'd only been thirty-six hours but even my own living room seemed bare and lonely. Why did it all feel so empty?

Chapter 10

My tires crunched over the gravel parking lot in front of the Taylors' veterinary hospital as I parked next to Brandon's SUV. I rarely stopped by his office, but I'd finished a meeting with a client at a nearby florist's and, on a whim, decided to pop by unannounced. If he hadn't seen his last patient yet, he would soon. The clinic closed in twenty minutes.

I took my phone and my keys and made my way to the front door. The bell tinkled happily when I walked inside, making Mrs. Taylor look up from her computer. "Jena! It's wonderful to see you, honey." She bustled around the counter to give me an enormous hug. "What brings you out here? Brandon didn't mention you'd stop by."

"I had an appointment with a client at that new florist up the road, so I thought I'd drop in to see him. Is he busy?"

She waved her hand dismissively. "Oh, he's just finishing up with vaccinating one of the police dogs, but he shouldn't be much longer." As Mrs. Taylor finished speaking and patted my arm, one of the exam rooms opened, and a muzzled German Shepherd led the way, followed by a uniformed police officer with Brandon behind him.

Brandon watched the dog as he walked toward the door. "The antihistamine I gave him should prevent a reaction this time, but if you notice any swelling, give us a call. One of us will meet you here to treat him." I stepped forward, and Brandon's head turned abruptly to me. A huge smile spread upon his face when he saw me.

"Thanks, doc."

He glanced back to the officer for a second. "Any time." The bell on the door rang as he strode forward and gave me a quick kiss on the cheek. "Not that I'm upset, but what are you doing here?"

"I was in the area. I thought you'd be off soon, so I thought I'd surprise you."

Brandon pointed at the police officer, who just re-entered without the dog to pay his bill. "I just finished with my last patient. Dad and I need to figure out who's on call tonight, but other than that, I'm free. What did you want to do?"

I shrugged and laughed. "I don't know. This was all kind of a spur of the moment thing."

The swinging door to the back of the clinic opened and Brandon's father strode out. "Mrs. Vernon just called about her cat, Cleo." Brandon shifted to the side as his father walked up. "Oh, I'm sorry. I didn't know you were here, Jena. How are you?"

"I'm good, thanks."

Brandon's forehead crinkled up with his frown. "What's wrong with Cleo?"

His father sighed. "Mrs. Vernon thinks he's been poisoned. He was fine this morning, but ever since he went outside, he's finished off his entire water bowl. Now, she says he's walking like he's drunk. He's also vomiting."

"Shit," said Brandon softly. "Do we have any antidote?"

"No, we used our only bottle on that schnauzer who came in last week. I ordered more but it hasn't arrived. It's just so rare to get two animals who've been exposed to antifreeze in such a short period of time around here. The antidote is also so expensive, I don't think Mrs. Vernon will be able to afford it."

Mrs. Taylor approached during the exchange. "I believe we ordered some pharmaceutical ethanol that should be in the delivery we received today. I'll go check."

Brandon's father nodded. "Yes, dear, thank you. We'll need to get that I.V. going as soon as she arrives."

I lifted my eyebrows. "Ethanol?"

Brandon's hand enveloped mine. "Ethanol is a good and inexpensive solution when you don't have the antidote. Like the prescription antidote, alcohol prevents the antifreeze from breaking down into toxic substances."

With the emergency coming in, I was in the way. "I should go."

"No," said Dr. Taylor. "The two of you should go do whatever it is you had planned. I can handle this."

Brandon scratched the back of his neck. "Dad, I—"

"I know you usually treat Cleo, but you have plans, and it's my night to be on call. Your mom will help me get the I.V. started. We'll order some dinner and eat it here. We'll probably bring Cleo home with us for monitoring. We'll be fine. Go."

"Are you sure?" Brandon's eyes held fast to his father.

"I'm positive," replied Dr. Taylor, "but you two need to hurry. You know how Mrs. Vernon is. She'll latch on to you when she walks in, and you'll never get away."

Brandon growled and squeezed my hand. "I feel guilty."

His father shook his head. "We always said we'd split on-call nights fifty-fifty, but you've taken more of the after-hours emergencies than I have since you were licensed. You've treated my patients while I slept or took your mother out for dinner. You've also been on call since you returned from Ellie's wedding almost two weeks ago. Take this one off." Dr. Taylor peered at me over his glasses. "Get him out of here and put a beer in his hand, so he's not tempted to come back."

"You'll call me."

His father rolled his eyes while he started pushing Brandon toward the door. "No, it's your night off. Tomorrow is my Saturday, so I'll let you know how it goes when you come for Sunday dinner."

"Dad," he said, drawing it out.

"Don't 'Dad' me. Take Jena out somewhere nice. Have some fun."

I started pulling Brandon's arm. "Do you have your keys and your phone?"

He put his hand in the pocket of his white coat. "Yes."

I drew him through the door and to his SUV. "I'll follow you to your house, then we'll decide what we're going to do."

Once I started my car, we drove a few miles out of town to the small house on his parents' acreage. They'd moved out of it years ago when they'd built a larger home further back by the lake. It was so long ago, I'd been out to the new house as much as the old one. Their property was far enough out of Marysville that Brandon usually drove to my place to spend the evening. More restaurants and things to do were available near the house.

He waited for me on the front porch, and we went inside together. Nothing had changed since the last time I'd been here. Mrs. Taylor's old sofa and recliner still occupied the living room, an old Formica table with mismatched chairs stood in the breakfast nook, and a workout bench took up the small dining room. Brandon hadn't added much in the way of decoration other than plaques he'd acquired while in the Army. His diplomas were in his exam room at the clinic.

"I should take a shower," he said, breaking the quiet.

I threw my purse and my keys on the sofa and wrapped my arms around his neck. "Do you want some help?"

His hands found my waist. "I'll never refuse such a generous offer, but if you want to go out tonight, you might want to wait here." He tugged at the scarf around my neck. "Are you still hiding that hickey?"

"It's taking forever to go away. At least it's a faint yellow today."

One side of his lips hooked upward into a boyish grin while he waggled his eyebrows. "Maybe I'll have to give you a new one. I think I'm going to miss that little spot. I was going to name it Fred if it lasted much longer."

"No, no more!" I stepped back from him. "You don't know how much grief I got from your sister, even in front of clients. She kept asking me why I wouldn't take off my scarf while she cackled. It'll only get worse when Ellie returns on Monday. Ellie won't be so indiscreet, but she'll still have a great time giving me grief."

He laced his fingers with mine and pulled me after him. "Talk to me while I take a shower."

I smiled as I trailed behind him into the bathroom. "Because you can't go without conversation for ten minutes?"

"No, because I've been without you since yesterday. I missed you." Brandon had an after-hours call for a colicky horse the prior evening. He'd had to leave nearly as soon as he'd arrived.

He removed his white coat, hanging it on the back of the door, before he peeled off his jeans and Polo shirt. Meanwhile, I'd hoisted myself to sit on the vanity so I could enjoy the show. All that was missing was a tub of popcorn. Of course, a glass of wine would be better.

"How was work?" he called out once he was under the running water.

"Spoke to a potential client this morning, but they have a meeting with another wedding planner tomorrow before they decide."

"They'll go with you. You're brilliant."

My heart expanded, filling my chest at his compliment. He always found some way to boost my ego when we talked. Of course, I'd always tried to compliment him when I had the chance. He'd always been a great guy and a great veterinarian. Sometimes, he simply needed reminding. We all need reminding of our strengths at times.

He'd been quiet for a moment, so I cocked my head slightly to one side and looked at the ceiling. "Are you wondering about Cleo?"

"I should've stayed."

"You can't be there every moment of every day. Your dad is an amazing vet, just like you are. Cleo is in good hands. You know that."

The curtain opened far enough for his head to pop out, his hair sudsy with shampoo. "I know, but Cleo's still very young. I've treated him since she first brought him in as a kitten."

"And it's hard to leave him to someone else."

"I feel like I'm abandoning him." His face was so solemn and serious.

"You're not. He has the best care possible. However, if you want to check in on him later, I won't be angry."

"Thanks," he said. The corners of his lips lifted just enough to take the forlorn appearance away.

I let out a breath and stretched my neck. "What do you want to do tonight? I think we should go out. If we stay in, you'll keep thinking about what's going on at the clinic."

"Dinner and a walk on the river? We could go to the end of the trail and watch the lightning bugs again, but this time, I want to kiss you if the mood strikes. You dodged me last time." He ducked behind the curtain. "Maybe we could share some ice cream too."

"Are we mimicking Lady and the Tramp? Are you going to want to share a huge bowl of spaghetti too?"

"The idea has definite possibilities." He pulled back the curtain and winked. "A little like the maple syrup at the resort."

My body jolted to life at the memory of him dripping the sticky syrup all over my body and licking it off. I'd had no choice that morning but to retaliate. When the syrup container was empty, we more than needed a shower, but we soaked in the Jacuzzi instead.

"I love making you blush." His grin grew wider. "You're always in such control. I like getting a reaction out of you." He disappeared behind the curtain, and the water slowed to a stop. When the curtain whipped open, my jaw went lax at the wet skin popsicle on display in front of me. Droplets rolled down his chest to his stomach and lower.

He covered himself with a towel, and after stepping out of the tub, lifted my chin with his knuckle. "If you keep looking at my dick like that, we won't be going anywhere for a long time."

"Do you have food in the refrigerator?"

His forehead furrowed. "No, why?"

"Then we're not staying here." I smiled, pushed him back, and slid from the counter. "I'm hungry and sex alone won't do it. You're going to have to feed me first." I stuck my tongue out and hurried from the bathroom before he could exact his revenge.

It wasn't long before he joined me in the living room. I was sitting on the sofa, checking my emails on my phone until he showed his handsome face. He wore his usual dark denim jeans with a forest green Henley that made his eyes look a lovely moss color.

"Are you ready?" he asked, fastening his watch.

"Where are we going? Do I need to change?" I held out my arms and looked at my navy slacks and white silk camisole. I had a blazer in the car, but the weather hadn't cooled enough for it yet.

"I don't think so." He wrapped an arm around me and pulled me to him. "You look beautiful."

My palms smoothed his shirt across his shoulders. "Have I ever told you how much I like this color on you?"

His head hitched back a fraction. "No. You do?"

I nodded while I watched my finger trail down his sternum. "Your eyes almost seem to change color with certain shades. Certain browns make them appear almost a wheat color. I believe Melanie described the shade as 'cured tobacco.' "

"Sounds like something out of a crappy romance novel." He watched my lips for a moment or two before he pressed a soft but simple kiss to them, lingering for a few seconds before he finally pulled away. "We should go. Do you have everything?"

"No," I said, pointing to the sofa. I let go of his hand so I could grab my purse and my keys before he led me out to his car. I nearly swooned on the spot when he opened my door. He was such a gentleman. Some women these days didn't appreciate those old-fashioned gestures, but I adored them. His manners were the icing on a very rich, decadent chocolate cake.

When he got in, I relaxed back into the seat while he started the car and headed into Marysville. We didn't talk, but the silence wasn't uncomfortable. Rather, it covered us more like a well-loved blanket.

As he parked, I couldn't help but smile. "The Garden? I haven't been here in forever."

"Is it okay? We can go somewhere else if you want."

"No, I hadn't even considered it. I've always loved this place, but I haven't been in ages."

He unbuckled and hurried around the car to open my door. Our fingers entwined as we walked through the gorgeous wrought iron gates. The Garden possessed an indoor dining room, but during nice weather, the tables outside became the main attraction. An array of potted plants and fairy lights lit the brick-paved alleyway lined with candlelit tables.

The hostess spotted us as we entered and hurried forward. She led us to a table in the back corner and left us with the evening's menus.

"When did you make the reservation?" I hadn't missed that he simply didn't request a table for two but, instead, gave a name at the hostess stand.

Brandon gave a modest one-shouldered shrug. "On the drive to my house. It's a Friday night in Marysville. You know as well as anyone who lives in this town; nice restaurants fill up quickly."

He was right. We had several wonderful places to eat in town, eliminating the need to drive into Charleston for a good meal. The problem was that our restaurants never failed to be packed solid on a Friday or Saturday evening.

The waiter appeared, took our drink order, and disappeared again.

"When do Ellie and William return?" he asked, sitting back in his chair.

"Tomorrow. We're grilling for dinner." I bit my bottom lip. "You're coming, aren't you?" I wasn't accustomed to asking a man out, but this *was* Brandon. My insides twisted and twirled pirouettes, but I didn't let that hold me back.

"Dad's covering the clinic. I'm free all day. I admit that I hoped we'd spend it together." His eyebrows lifted on his forehead as his hand found mine under the table. We weren't seated so much across from each other as we were beside one another, facing out toward the rest of the diners.

"That sounds nice. Did you have anything special in mind?"

His fingers trailed up and down the back of my hand to my wrist, making me a bit dizzy. "Not really. If you have any errands to run or need to go out, I'll drive you. Other than that, just a lazy day to sit around and relax."

"That sounds nice," I said. Our waiter set my glass of wine in front of me and Brandon's beer in front of him. While we had the waiter's attention, we made quick decisions on our dinner, so he could put our order in to the kitchen before the rest of the diners.

We talked about whatever came to mind until our food came. The conversation didn't falter as we ate, either. When the waiter came back around and took our plates, he glanced back and forth between us. "Can I interest you in dessert? The chef has prepared an incredible bourbon apple pecan bread pudding for tonight. It's served with a scoop of homemade vanilla ice cream and covered in a bourbon sauce that is out of this world."

How did the waiter know the perfect dessert for Brandon? That man loved bread pudding and apple pie was no sloppy second.

As if on command, Brandon said, "Oooh. Share that with me." His hopeful eyes bore into me while his hand squeezed mine. He always had such a sweet tooth! "Come on. You know you want to."

I pointed at him with my free hand. "*You* have to run with me in the morning."

"Deal!" He nodded at the waiter and leaned over to claim my lips. "Thank you."

I kissed him until he pulled back to his seat. We didn't have to wait long for the dessert to be placed between us with two spoons. Brandon swiftly picked up his and took a bite, then he loaded the spoon and put it in front of me. "Your turn."

When the bread pudding hit my tongue, the buttery concoction melted in my mouth and mingled with the ice cream. I sighed and relaxed. "It's incredible." I opened my eyes, meeting a very familiar pair of brown eyes staring at me from another table. I cleared my throat and naturally shifted closer to Brandon.

If someone had asked me the day before whether seeing Connor Willoughby would upset me, I would've said yes, but oddly, I felt nothing—no hurt, no anger. I took my spoon and started dishing up my next bite.

"Jen?" Brandon peered over at Connor and back at me. Instead of eating that next spoonful myself, I shoved it in Brandon's open mouth and giggled at his surprise. He smiled and swallowed once he'd chewed a few times. "Are you okay?"

"I'm fine."

"Pinky swear?" He held out his pinky, and I chuckled while I linked my little finger with his.

"Yeah, pinky swear."

Brandon looked back, but I took another bite of ice cream while I tapped my knee against his. "Hey, I'm over here."

He paused in scooping another bit of bread pudding. "Did you think I'd forgotten?"

"I just wanted to make sure." I brushed my leg against his.

"I could never forget about you."

"You better not," I said. I dragged the spoon out of my mouth slowly, deliberately. "Of course, if you keep staring other places, I might just eat the entire dessert all by myself."

He cleared his throat and chuckled. "No way." He dug in. "Because you'd still expect me to run with you in the morning."

"You know I would."

The dessert didn't last long, so once Brandon paid the bill, we walked to the sidewalk and headed in the direction of the river.

"Why don't we go home?" I asked. One of my hands held his while the opposite wrapped around his arm. "We can curl up on the sofa, watch a movie, or talk while we listen to music. I don't care."

His fingers trailed down my cheek. "Are you sure?"

"Positive," I said. "I love the lightning bugs, but we can do that another day. I'd rather be alone with you."

We loaded into the car, and when it pulled into the driveway at my house, I peered up at the balcony. "I'm surprised you didn't take me to your place."

"I've made a few improvements to my house, but ultimately, it belongs to my parents, and they'll rent it to someone new whenever I choose to move out. It's not home. I'd rather be here . . . with you."

Something in my stomach flip-flopped and made my heart stutter. "Oh." Other than that, my mind was blank. Why couldn't I have thought of a better word? He must have thought I sounded like an idiot.

Fortunately, Brandon never commented while he helped me out of the car, and I followed him up the stairs. I unlocked the door, and he turned on the lights while I disarmed the alarm system. I plopped my purse and my keys on a small table near the balcony door, then wrapped my arms around Brandon from behind.

"Why don't you call your dad? You can check in on Cleo while I change out of my work clothes." I kissed between his shoulder blades. "I'll be right back." While I made my way to my room, his phone beeped as he dialed. He started speaking as I closed the door behind me.

I dug through one of my drawers until I found a matching camisole and panty set. It was simple cotton and not necessarily sexy, but other than what I'd bought for the bridesmaid dress, I didn't own lacey lingerie. This was it. Take it or leave it. This was me.

Before I could change my mind, I stripped, put on the pajamas, and tossed my work clothes in the hamper before I tiptoed back through the door.

Brandon sat on the sofa nodding while he held the phone to his ear. I managed to make it around the stairs that led down to the office and behind him without him noticing me. As I approached him from behind, he let out a heavy breath. "I can't think of anything you haven't done. Hopefully, it works before his kidneys are permanently damaged . . . Call me if you need me. Thanks, Dad . . . Bye."

He removed the phone from his ear and looked at the screen as I crept closer. I put my hands on his shoulders, making him jump. I dug my thumbs into the tight muscles of his upper back and kneaded.

"How is he?"

"Drunk but holding his own at the moment." He groaned, and his head dropped back to rest against the cushions, his eyes closed. "It's difficult because we don't know when he ingested the anti-freeze. We're also assuming the poison based on his symptoms. The problem is you have to treat ethylene glycol poisoning quickly, so we don't have time to test him for it. By the time we got the results back, it would be too late."

"Do you test them anyway?"

"I'm sure Dad took some blood and will send it off tomorrow. We still won't know anything until Monday." His eyes opened and met mine. "Are we going to talk about Connor Willoughby?"

My fingers paused. "Why would we do that?"

"Since the two of you broke up, he's always upset you and—"

"Well, he didn't tonight. He was just another person, and I don't want to ruin our evening talking about him."

"He didn't bother you?" His eyebrows sat high on his forehead.

"Seeing him there surprised me too, but no." I walked around the end of the sofa and straddled his lap. "I'd much rather talk about anything but Connor—or we don't have to talk at all."

His eyes roved over my tank to where it left a tiny portion of my stomach uncovered, then further to the matching panties. "You do know how to make an impression."

"It's nothing fancy." I wrapped my arms around his neck and lightly bit his neck.

He sucked in a breath and his grip on my thighs tightened. "I'm not saying I wouldn't enjoy lace or satin, but I don't need them. I just need you."

Chapter 11

The clock on the bedside table read seven when my eyes sprang open. Every morning, out of habit, I woke about that same time. I did have the rare day where I slept late; however, those days were few and far between.

I nestled closer to Brandon and sighed. The few men I'd slept with had never been cuddlers, so I never realized I'd enjoy spending the night in someone's arms so much. Brandon lay on his back while I curled up to his side with my leg thrown over his hip. My head rested on his shoulder just above his chest, though his heart still beat loudly in my ear, the soothing drumbeat that had lulled me into the land of Nod. My hand rested on his chest, but my thumb caressed the light spattering of hair that tapered down his stomach and disappeared under the sheet.

Last night, we'd kissed and touched on the sofa like a couple of horny teenagers. We were barely dressed by the time he stood, wrapping my legs around his waist so he could carry me to bed. One thing about Brandon Taylor I hadn't known before we became intimate—he was far from a stingy lover. He loved touching me and coaxing me to a mind-splitting orgasm until I begged him to finally come into me. Just the thought of how sensitive and achy he'd made me whenever we made love made me tightly clench my thighs for some relief—even now.

Carefully, I lifted onto my forearm. He appeared so much younger and relaxed while he slept. I leaned down and softly kissed his shoulder, then his chest. When he didn't so much as twitch, I pressed my lips to the side of his ribs, running my palm over his hip. His breathing remained steady, even though his cock had noticeably started to awaken as I kissed him. He must've tuckered himself out last night for that to be his only reaction.

On a whim, I ducked under the covers and took his length in my mouth. A loud gasp split the silence, but I wrapped my hand around the part I couldn't fit and stroked the soft skin while I sucked. His hips lifted as the sheet and quilt were thrown to the other side of the bed.

"Jesus, Jena. I can . . . I can't." His eyes rolled back in his head as it flopped back on to the pillow, the knuckles on his one hand white from clenching the sheets, pulling them away from the mattress. The other hand found my hair, burying his fingers. Watching his breathing increase and watching him lose more and more of his control was the sexiest thing I'd ever seen. When we made love, he always exhibited so much control over his own body. I loved that I could reduce him to nothing more than a writhing, moaning mess.

His hand began to tug on my hair like he was trying to drag me on top of him, but I resisted. "Jena, please." The whimper only made me more desperate to finish him like this, so instead of giving in to him, I sucked harder and increased the pace.

He swore and vocalized something unintelligible on every exhale until he finally gave a guttural cry and came. After one last shudder, he succeeded and pulled me over him.

"I should brush—" His mouth clamped over mine before I could tell him I should brush my teeth. He pressed me flush to his chest while I straddled his legs and kissed him back, my tongue dueling with his until he gentled the exchange. His lips brushed mine softly once, then twice.

"That was one hell of a wake up." He kissed where my neck and shoulder met.

"You liked it?"

"You couldn't tell?" he asked with a laugh. I shrugged and played with his chest hair, not able to look him in the eye, until he tipped my chin up, suddenly serious. "You don't need to doubt yourself with me. I only want you to be yourself when we're together."

"I've never done that before."

"Really?" He had this proud as a peacock grin that made me want to pinch him. Instead, I only nodded and kissed him soundly on the lips.

"I wanted to do it. I actually liked it. It was awesome watching you lose yourself."

He grinned and lifted his eyebrows. "I imagine it's not too different from how I enjoy watching you." His strong fingers kneaded my thighs. "If you give me a bit of time, I'll make it up to you."

I shook my head and pulled away. "I don't expect anything in return." I grazed my teeth over my bottom lip. "But I won't turn you down later if you're in the mood." I grabbed his hands and started hoisting him from the bed. "In the meantime, you said you'd run with me this morning."

"You expect me to jog now? After that? I'm ready for a nice, long nap."

"Come on. You're the one who ordered that bread pudding. You promised."

I took my clothes out of my dresser and rummaged on the shelf in my closet, finding a pair of his running shorts, underwear, and a t-shirt from when we ran the Marysville 5K a few months ago. That day, he'd showered at my house. I'd washed his sweaty clothes but had forgotten to give them back. His running shoes were shoved to the far recesses of my closet floor.

"That's where those went," he said when I tossed them into his lap.

"We can run by your house and get you a change of clothes later if you want."

He pulled on his boxer briefs as he stood. "After Monday night, I packed a bag and put it in the back of my car." When I looked up, he watched me as though I might explode. "I was late for work. Dad wasn't mad but he kept laughing at me all morning."

"If you wore that stupid grin you wore when you left, he probably guessed what you'd been up to all night. Did he know you came over here?"

"No, but I live on his property, so he knew I wasn't home all night. He would've noticed my car wasn't there when he and mom went home that evening as well as when they left the next morning." Brandon put on his shorts and t-shirt before drawing me close to him. "I wonder if he realizes it's you."

I combed my fingers through his short hair, trying unsuccessfully to fix his bed head. "Based on how hard he was shoving you out the door last night, he might have some idea. Were you trying to hide us?"

"No, but I didn't go announcing it either. I guess I wanted to let both of us settle into this first. Having Ellie and William away for the last two weeks has given us a lot of time on our own. Charlie has made herself scarce as well. As for Dad, I've been working a lot in the past few months. He might've just wanted me to have a night off." He kissed my forehead before he grabbed a worn baseball cap from the bedside table. I'd always had his belongings all over the house. The major difference lately was that he was here with them. "Where do you want to run?"

"How about through the park to the running trail that follows the river. We can stop when we reach the old water wheel and head back."

"That's a long run," he said. "When did you start taking that route?"

"I swap my runs around, so I'm always taking a different trail. I don't like to be predictable. When I take that path, I stop running at the end of the river trail on the way back. That makes five miles. Then, I walk home to cool down."

"Sounds good." He looked down to my breasts and laughed. "I'm definitely not complaining, but when are you going to get dressed?"

I shoved him hard. "I would've before now if you hadn't distracted me."

Throwing on my workout clothes only took a few minutes, so not too much time had passed before we were locking the door behind us and setting out. Brandon was a faster runner. We usually ran races at our own paces, but today, he didn't leave me behind. A number of other runners passed us with earbuds on, but I never ran with music unless I was on a treadmill at the gym. I liked to hear what was going on around me—the sounds of nature or even an oncoming car.

Our feet pounded against the pavement as we followed the winding sidewalk that headed toward the river. At the bridge, instead of going right to the shops, we turned left and took the dirt path that followed the water all the way to the old mill, not talking until we'd double backed to the bridge and began walking to cool down. The bright blue sky, puffy clouds, and cool breeze enticed us to stretch in the park before we went home. The soft grass with the pleasant weather made for a better atmosphere than a yoga mat on the floor of the living room.

We showered and couldn't resist soaping each other, which of course, led to other enjoyable activities. Once we dressed, Brandon ushered me to a chair at the table while he made me blueberry pancakes for breakfast. One thing about this relationship—I was going to weigh a ton if he kept feeding me like this!

After we'd cleaned up, we spent a lazy afternoon relaxing in the hammock in the backyard. We cuddled, we talked, we read books we'd brought down with us. We simply enjoyed the beautiful day and being with each other.

I don't know when I fell asleep, but the next thing I knew, the sound of crunching leaves permeated the fog in my head and pulled me from whatever dream my mind had conjured—not that I remembered it. I blinked as Brandon's chest rose and fell in an even rhythm under my cheek. Since he still slept, I carefully sat up from where I lay sprawled partially over him and almost fell out of the hammock when Ellie appeared a few feet away, her eyebrows high enough to disappear under her hair.

As soon as I was on my feet, I grabbed Ellie's arm and dragged her through the gate to her own backyard. "When did you get home?"

"A couple of hours ago. I slept while William and Freya went grocery shopping. Now, Freya is napping, so I thought I'd check to see if we're still on for dinner." She crossed her arms over her chest. "When did you and Brandon hook up?"

"You act as though we've never slept in the same bed before," I said with a huff.

"Yes, but I doubt his hand cupped your ass then like it did just now." She grinned and threw a foot out. "Does Charlie know?"

"We'd decided to take things slow and start dating right before your wedding." I watched my big toe trace circles in the grass. "That sort of changed at the reception, and yes, Charlie knows. She told me she'd kick my ass if I hurt him."

I startled when Ellie put her hands on my upper arms. "Good! It's about time the two of you finally jumped into the deep end. How do you feel?"

A high-pitched laugh burst out. "Like I'm standing right on the edge of a high cliff."

Ellie lifted that one eyebrow she favored. "Have you ever felt that way before?"

"No," I said with a jerk of my head. "This is terrifying."

"Yes," she said, making a fist and jerking her elbow back at her side. "That's a good thing. That fear means whatever exists between you and Brandon is real."

"Ellie, I'm so impulsive lately. I went to the vet clinic yesterday because I couldn't wait to see him. Every evening, unless he has an after-hours call, we're together. Sometimes, we meet for lunch too. It's so unlike me."

"Why? Because you've always had to control everything? Love isn't something you can predict or curb. Sometimes it's a slow burn, and other times, it's overwhelming the speed at which it takes hold and engulfs you. With William, I felt like I was racing along at a hundred and fifty miles an hour. When I answered that phone call from his wife, I may as well have slammed full speed into a brick wall. I'd tried to keep a handle on how I felt, but I couldn't. Why do you think I fought so hard against him when I discovered I was pregnant? I fell so hard and so fast."

My fingers fidgeted. "That's part of what's terrifying. I know I'm falling in love with him."

"Have you told him that?"

"No, we only started this less than two weeks ago. It's too soon, isn't it?"

Ellie shrugged her shoulders. "I fell in love with William in less time than that. I just hadn't recognized it for what it was. But, I'd just met William. You've known Brandon your entire life. He's your best friend. You've always told him everything. It doesn't surprise me that your feelings would deepen quickly."

I gnawed at my lip and gripped my hands together. "We bumped into Connor last night."

She sucked air through her teeth and winced. "How did that go?"

"I looked at him and, honestly, wished him away. He didn't bother me, but I didn't want him to bother us, if that makes sense. Brandon worried about me. I told him I didn't feel anything for Connor, but I'm not sure he believed me."

"Brandon knows everything," said Ellie. "He might see Connor as competition—"

My stomach clenched. "But he's not. I don't want Connor back."

"Maybe you need to reassure Brandon? Tell him you're falling in love with him. Neither of you should have insecurities if you're open with each other."

"Ellie!"

We both turned at Brandon's voice. He strode forward and wrapped my little sister in a hug and rocked her back and forth before stepping back. "How was the honeymoon?"

"We had a lot of fun. Freya adored Disney World and there was always something to do."

"I bet. I hope you took some amazing photos—especially ones of the tiny munchkin with the characters."

A laugh bubbled from Ellie's lips. "We could bore you for days with those."

Brandon's arm wrapped around my waist, and I propped my chin on his shoulder.

"Ellie came over to see if we're still on for tonight."

"Definitely." He glanced at his watch and started. "I didn't realize it was so late. Maybe we should walk to the grocery store. The refrigerator is pretty bare after breakfast."

Ellie waved her hand dismissively. "We bought a ton of food. You don't necessarily have to go now."

"Thanks," I said with a wave of my hand, "but we're out of some basics, so we do need to make a grocery run."

Brandon yawned. "Maybe a cup of coffee too. I need to wake up. I can't believe I slept for two hours. I guess we got less sleep last night than I thought."

One side of Ellie's lips curved up into an impish expression. "How much did you sleep last night, Jena?"

My cheeks burned so hotly, it might as well have been summer. "We're going. We'll be back at four?"

"Sounds good. I figured we'd eat at five."

Before Brandon could embarrass me further, I pushed him toward the gate but didn't say a word until we began climbing the steps to the balcony. "Did you have to bring up how much we slept last night?"

"What? We agreed we weren't keeping things a secret. Besides, I could've said I was tired because you kept me up last night."

My fingers located a sensitive spot on his ribs and delivered a hard pinch. "I would've said we kept each other awake."

"More like I couldn't sleep because of all the yelling and groaning you did." His lop-sided grin was adorable and sexy as hell and frustrating all at the same time. How did he do that?

I propped my hands on my hips. "And why was that? I wasn't giving myself an orgasm."

His hand reached out and clasped my side. "God, I'd love to watch that." His eyes had grown serious and had dropped to my body instead of my face.

Pulling his hands from me, I started walking up the last few steps backward, my finger held up in front of me. "No, we have to go to the store."

"I can be fast."

An incredulous bark erupted from my throat. "Hearing that is such a turn on."

When my foot cleared the top step, I turned tail and ran with a squeal, barely making it in the door before he caught me. With an arm around my waist, he easily scooped me up and hauled me into his arms. I didn't even have time to wrestle my way free since he pressed me against the wall and pushed his hips into mine. I should've known he'd be ready to go.

"You can't leave me like this."

"Well, I wouldn't want you to claim I kept you from eating when we have no food." I kept my voice light while I struggled to keep from giggling.

His lips started an assault on my neck and worked their way up until he kissed me like he was starved for me. That familiar ache began to build, but instead of giving myself over to it, I gentled the kiss and pulled away, managing to slip to one side for a quick escape. "We should go." I snagged the re-useable shopping bags hanging from a hook on the wall. "What do you want for breakfast tomorrow?"

He just stood there, staring at me slack jawed, then he blinked. "You want to go now?"

"Uh-huh."

I slung my purse over my shoulder and started down the stairs toward the front door. "Are you coming?"

As I neared the bottom step, his footfalls suddenly followed. "No, that's the problem." His voice was low and grumbly. I bet if I peered back, he'd be pouting like a little boy. I gave in to temptation and took a peek, giggling when I saw him. He did wear a pout, and his hands were shoved into his pockets, making him look like the boy I remember from so long ago. He was so adorable that I wanted to muss his hair.

I waited for him by the door and leaned against his side to whisper in his ear, "I'll make it up to you later."

Dinner that night was wonderful. The food was cooked to perfection, the wine was delicious, and my sister and William weren't just good company—they were the best. I also grew more comfortable with Brandon's little gestures of affection in front of Ellie and William over the course of the evening. When Brandon first kissed me in front of them, I'd frozen in place, even though it was nothing more than a peck. By the end of the evening, we cuddled in front of the fire pit while we all chatted. It was like it'd always been that way.

When we returned to the house, I put the pan of leftovers in the fridge and stretched once the door closed. Like earlier, Brandon's arms snaked around me from behind and drew me back against his strong body, making parts of my body roar to life.

"Are you tired?" His low voice rumbled in my ear and my eyes fluttered closed.

"Exhausted," I said. I pressed my lips together while I waited for him to retaliate.

His fingers dug into my ribs, and I involuntarily burst into laughter. "Really? You're that tired?"

I twisted from his grip and ran as fast as I could into the bedroom. He picked me up when he reached me and pressed me down into the mattress, my hands pinned above my head.

"How tired?"

"Who said I was tired? I'm wide awake."

"That was what I thought you said." His lips began an onslaught on my neck that progressed to much more. When he finally groaned in release and covered me, my arms joined my legs to wrap around him, holding him close.

My heart beat like it wanted to escape from my ribs, my flesh burned from every touch as though his hands still stroked my skin, and I wanted desperately to hold him to me and never let go. I didn't know how I wasn't shaking violently from head to toe. I'd told Ellie I felt like I was standing on the edge of a cliff, but something had changed. The cliff had disappeared. I'd swan dived right into an abyss of everything that was just as messy and terrifying.

Tears leaked from my eyes, I kissed his hair, and I took a deep breath. "I love you," I said against his ear.

He lifted himself onto his forearms, so his face remained close to mine, his eyes searching—delving for the honest truth of my words. "Say it again."

"I love you." My teeth grazed over my bottom lip while I waited for his reaction.

With a heart-stopping smile, he dropped down and brushed his lips against mine. When his eyes opened again, he steadily held my gaze. "I love you too."

Chapter 12

Brandon opened the door of the church and propelled me inside first by our joined hands. We were late! The opening hymn could be heard through the inner doors to the sanctuary. As I approached, Brandon pulled the handle, and I tiptoed to the rear of the aisle.

Fortunately, my father always sat to the back of the church, and today was no different. He held down his normal pew with Melanie to the outside and Ellie sitting on his opposite side. William held Freya on his lap.

Dad looked up as we neared, and he and Melanie stood, so we could squeeze in while Ellie and William scooted down, so we had a place to sit.

Our families had attended the same church for forever, but while the Barretts always sat to the back, the Taylors occupied the pew at the very front. I never knew why. It was just one of those crazy family traditions no one ever questioned. It was simply how it had always been.

When the service ended, I kissed my dad on the cheek before I followed Brandon to where his parents were rising from their seats.

"Hi, Mom," he said, giving his mother a big hug.

"You're coming for Sunday dinner, aren't you?" His mother gave him such a hopeful look that guilt skittered up my spine. We'd been spending so much time together that he hadn't spent a few Sundays with his family.

He peered back at me. "Jena and I are both coming, if that's okay?"

I leaned forward and hugged his mom. "Hi, Mrs. Taylor."

"Of course, it's okay!" she said as she held my arms. "Jena hasn't come for Sunday dinner in ages. It'll be nice to catch up." She hit her husband's arm. "Don't forget we need to stop by the store for milk and bread before we go home. We'll need to hurry."

"Mom," said Brandon before his dad could answer, "Jena and I can do that on our way."

Her eyes perked up. "Are you sure?"

"Positive," I said, nodding. "I'm certain you'll want to get dinner going as soon as you get home. You've always made such wonderful Sunday meals." My mother's Sunday cooking endeavors had always been out of a box—add a pound of ground meat and voila, you had an instant meal.

"Oh, aren't you sweet." She waved off my compliment. "I'm a huge fan of my slow cooker. I get that going early Sunday morning, so all I have to do is make a salad and some bread. Today, I made Brandon's favorite."

Brandon perked up and rubbed his hands together eagerly. "Lasagna?" His arm wrapped around my shoulders. "We should hurry, Jen. I don't want Charlie to get there first and eat all of it."

His sister, who stood by his father with her hands shoved into her pockets, rolled her eyes. "Oh, please! How can I eat it all when I always have to fight you just for one serving?"

"Alright, children," said Mr. Taylor with a wink in my direction. "I don't know about the rest of you, but I'm not in the mood to stay here for coffee and cookies. I'd rather go home and have a real meal."

Mrs. Taylor elbowed her husband in the ribs. "You mean you want to turn on football."

Brandon laughed. "Yes, we do." He glanced over at me. "Are you ready?" I wasn't surprised. In the Taylor household, Sundays in the fall always consisted of a meal, football, and for the men, beer.

His hand dropped from my shoulder to entwine his fingers with mine as he led me outside. Charlie headed to the Taylor's car with her parents while I climbed into Brandon's SUV. The store was located around the corner, so it wasn't long before we walked into the over-air-conditioned building, making me shiver.

A stand of flowers stood centered to the doors as customers walked in, and I stepped forward, surveying the selection. I'd never gone to Brandon's boyhood home as his girlfriend. Should I bring flowers to his mom this time? It was possible his father had some idea about us, but how much did they actually know? Had they just assumed we were still merely friends? Would they dislike how our relationship had changed?

"What are you doing?" he said near my ear.

"I should get your mom some flowers."

He rubbed my back and kissed my temple. "You've never thought to bring her flowers before. Are you suddenly nervous?"

I'd been biting my fingernail, so I stopped, flopping my hands down to my sides. "Yeah, I guess. It was one thing when we were friends. What if I'm not what your mom wanted for her little boy?"

"Then, hopefully, she'll keep her mouth shut." He chuckled while he said it. "I love my parents, but it's my life. I'm going to be with whom I want. She's never pressed me about a certain woman in the past. To be honest, I don't think she's ever given it that much thought." I lifted a bouquet of lilies, but Brandon put a hand on mine. "If you want to bring my mom flowers, buy her the roses or the tulips."

"Why?"

"Because we have cats, and lilies are often poisonous."

I quickly returned the lilies to their bucket before I selected a pretty cluster of pink and white roses. When I turned to Brandon, I held them out to him. "What do you think? Neither are in season, but tulips are never so nice from the hothouse."

"I think she'll love them." He glanced toward the aisles. "Why don't I grab the milk and the bread while you go pick out some wine? Mom didn't mention she needed any, but Dad, Charlie, and I will drink beer while we watch the game. I thought you might want a glass of something."

"Okay," I said as I backed away from him. I waited until I was slowly turning to say, "Don't be long. I'll be waiting for you."

I could hear his low chuckle as I sashayed off, peering down at my watch. The question was how long would it take for him to find me in the alcohol section?

When I reached the wine, beer, and liquor, I started down the row but saw Connor not five steps away and immediately tried pivoting on my heel to make a quick escape. Maybe there were some bottles on sale at the end of the aisle?

"Jena!"

My eyes squeezed closed while I groaned inside. Why was he insisting on speaking to me now? I'd avoided him because I didn't want to be rude. Now that he'd given me no other choice, I faced him and forced a smile. "Hello, Connor."

His eyes roved me up and down, making me want to pull my sweater over my black sheath dress. "You're looking well."

"Thanks. I hope you're doing okay." I wouldn't give him the satisfaction of giving him the once over he gave me.

"I'm fine." He cleared his throat and peered down to the bottle of liquor in his hands. "Lacy and I broke up."

"I'm so sorry." Was I truly sorry? Not in the slightest.

One side of his lips quirked up. "I should've known you'd say that. You don't have a mean bone in your body, do you?"

I sighed and walked around him to the red wines. "I'm human, just like everyone else, so I'm not sure what you mean by that. I would never want to hurt anyone's feelings—not intentionally anyway."

He followed me over to the shelf. "I'd love to talk to you sometime. Could I give you a call?"

I clasped two bottles of my favorite Chianti to my chest. "I've moved on, Connor. I'm happy. I think you should find someone who makes you happy since that woman wasn't me."

Before he could get another word out of his mouth, I strode as fast as I could around him and in the direction of the bakery. I wasn't going to wait for Brandon while Connor lingered and pestered me. Besides, who in the hell did that man think he was? The asshole cheated on me, and now, he wanted to patch things up? I could just hear Charlie's rant on that development.

Luckily, I practically ran into Brandon when I rounded the corner. "You've got the bread?" I asked. He held up two large loaves of French bread. "Great, let's go."

His forehead furrowed and he peered over my shoulder. "What's wrong?"

"We'll talk in the car. Let's get out of here."

We joined the line at the express lane and put our purchases on the belt. Brandon had just set down the bread when Connor stepped up behind us. "Taylor," he said with a nod.

Brandon scowled and peered back at me without responding to Connor's greeting—not that I blamed him in the slightest. I took Brandon's hand and drew him closer to me. The last thing I wanted was a three-act drama to go down in the middle of the largest grocery store in Marysville after church. The entire town stopped in at that time. With that crowd, no one would have to hear the gossip; they'd witness the event first-hand.

As our purchases were scanned, I pulled a couple of compact reusable bags from my purse and loaded everything up while Brandon paid. As soon as we were back in the car, he used the steering wheel to pivot around to face me. "What did he do?"

"It's stupid. I don't know why he even spoke to me. Let's just go and forget about it."

"He must've said something, though. You wouldn't have practically run from the place if he hadn't." His eyes scanned mine, searching for more than I was saying.

I took his cheeks in my hands. "Look at me. I don't care what Connor Willoughby says. If you have to know, he asked if we could talk sometime. I told him I'd moved on and he should too."

His jaw clenched and released under my palms. "I know he hurt you. Are you sure—?"

"I'm positive," I said, willing him to believe me. "I told you I love you, and I meant every word. Now, we were going to have a nice day with your family. I don't want Connor to spoil it. Do you?"

"No, I'm sorry. I shouldn't have gone all caveman on you."

I laughed and sat back so he could start the car. "That was caveman? You hardly clubbed him and dragged me off." The smile he gave me wasn't quite his normal cheerful one, but it was certainly better than the tension from earlier. "I love you," I said. Maybe saying it again would help remedy his worry.

His shoulders released their tension, and he leaned across to place a quick kiss to my lips. "I love you too."

When we arrived at his parents' house, he carried the bag and the bread while I took the flowers. He walked straight through the front door without knocking. "Mom! We're here!" The rich scent of tomato sauce, garlic, and melted cheese hit my nose the moment I stepped foot into the foyer, making my stomach growl. I hadn't exaggerated when I complimented Mrs. Taylor's Sunday dinners. They were the best.

I trailed behind Brandon to the homey kitchen where he set the bags on the island. How many times had I sat at the bar and eaten cookies or a snack before Brandon and I scampered outside to play?

"We've got your groceries." He took the milk and put it in the refrigerator while his mother unwrapped and began cutting the French bread.

"As soon as the garlic bread is done, we'll be ready to eat," she said. When she glanced over at me, she smiled. "What beautiful roses!"

Brandon put his arm around his mom's shoulders. "Jena picked those out for you."

Mrs. Taylor started and set down the knife. "Why, you didn't have to do that." She hurried over to a china cabinet on one wall and pulled out a cut-glass vase. "It's so sweet of you, but you know you don't ever have to bring anything but yourselves when you come to dinner. Would you be a dear and arrange them for me? They'll be pretty on the dining room table."

While I unwrapped the stems, Brandon took a beer from the fridge and, after opening a drawer, set a pair of scissors on the counter next to me.

"Thank you."

He leaned in and kissed me softly on the lips, lingering for a moment. I sure as heck hadn't expected him to tell his parents in quite that way. A fire may as well have engulfed me at that moment. Lord, I was probably as red as a tomato! He grinned when he drew back. "I'll be in the living room with Dad if you need anything."

I licked my lips and concentrated on those flowers like they would solve the world's most pressing problems. Only the sound of the French bread crunching as his mother worked filled the room.

"Now I understand the flowers," she said quietly. "You're here today as Brandon's girlfriend and not his childhood best friend. I don't know how I missed the change except that the two of you have always been so close, holding hands and such since you were kids."

When I finally gathered the courage to look at her, she chuckled and stepped over, taking my hands. "Sweetie, relax! You practically grew up in my kitchen as much as Brandon grew up in yours. I want nothing more than my children to be healthy and happy—and that includes you. You and Ellie are a part of this family too."

"Thank you. I'm sorry if I'm not myself. I guess it's awkward."

"I can understand that." She wiped her hands on a towel and picked up a bottle of wine. "I'm glad y'all thought to bring this." Once she poured two glasses, she pushed one across the counter. "Now, I want you to tell me what's been going on at that business of yours. You always have the best stories. Mind, I don't spread them around, but Dr. Taylor and I do enjoy some of the more ridiculous ones."

She took a sip of wine and lifted her perfectly waxed eyebrows. And, just like that, Mrs. Taylor ignored everything else and treated me no differently from the way she had all my life.

As always, Mrs. Taylor's lasagna didn't disappoint, and despite her protests, I helped clean up while Charlie, Brandon, and their dad settled in for the game. When the dishwasher was running, I joined Brandon on the sofa with a glass of wine, pulling my feet up under me.

He took my hand. "You okay?" His lips pressed against mine.

"Good lord! Don't tell me that now I have to put up with PDA from the two of you too? There are places for that, you know—like the hall, the bedrooms . . . you know, private places."

"Thanks, Charlie," said Brandon. "Remind me to embarrass you when the time comes."

"When did this happen?" We turned to Dr. Taylor whose eyes darted back and forth between us.

Brandon's brows dipped in the middle. "I figured you knew. You practically shoved us out of the door before Cleo arrived the other night."

"You're always on-call, and the two of you obviously had plans. I was glad to give you the night off. I've noticed the two of you holding hands a lot lately, but you've held hands since you were three. How was I supposed to guess it was different this time?"

I took the last sip of my wine and set my empty glass on the coffee table as Mrs. Taylor walked in with a glass casserole dish and plates. "I have caramel chocolate turtle dump cake if anyone wants dessert. I've also brewed a pot of coffee." She placed the dessert on the coffee table and stood. "Why's it so quiet in here?"

Dr. Taylor pointed at us from his recliner. "Did you know they're now a couple?"

"Not until today." She scooped some cake onto a plate and handed it to her husband along with a fork. "Frankly, I'm relieved. He hasn't brought home a girl since high school." She looked over her glasses at us. "Not that I'm in a hurry, but

Charlie hasn't brought home a boy since Jensen. I've been ready for grandchildren for the past few years. I would prefer you to marry first, though."

Brandon's chest and shoulders shook as he took a sip of his beer. "We'll keep that in mind, Mom."

I couldn't pass up the dessert, and after the wine and all of the food, I had trouble keeping my eyes open. The next thing I knew, a hand to my shoulder shook me gently and someone kissed my nose. "Wake up, sleepyhead."

My eyes fluttered and blinked several times, needing a moment to focus on Brandon's face. "How long have I been asleep?"

"About three hours," he said, helping me up. "Are you ready to go home?"

I nodded. "Are you okay to drive?"

"I only had two beers. My last was when you fell asleep. I'm fine."

My arms wrapped around his shoulders, and I buried my face in his neck. "Good. Let's go home."

Chapter 13

Nearly three weeks flew by as Brandon and I spent every evening together. For the most part, he'd moved into my place even though some of his furniture and clothes still remained at his house. Not that we'd made moving in together an official thing—it'd just sort of happened. When he wasn't on-call or I didn't have a wedding, we spent our evenings cuddled on the couch watching television or reading. When he had to care for a patient after-hours, he returned to my house, just as when I had a wedding, he waited for me at my place until I finished.

At the risk of sounding totally corny, I fell deeper and deeper in love with him by the day, hour, minute, and second. For the life of me, I couldn't understand why I'd been so resistant to the idea in the first place. Ellie had been right. All this time, I'd been searching for Brandon—for what I had with him—in other relationships. We knew one another, we shared everything about ourselves, and we loved one another for the contents of our hearts. Thank goodness, Ellie had completely freaked me out and made me see what I'd been missing for years.

After one last spray of perfume, I stood back and checked my appearance in the full-length mirror hanging on my closet door. Today was not only Friday, but it was also Brandon's birthday, and of course, I'd planned a special evening. He had absolutely no clue, either, only that I'd told him to pick me up at five when the office closed.

I'd put my hair into a low loose bun with a few curled tendrils left free to frame my face, I'd bought a sexy black dress, and my freshly shaven legs looked amazing with the crazy high pair of strappy, black stilettos I wore.

Yep, I had big plans! First, I was going to take my man out for his favorite steak before I brought him back and showed him the new black lace get-up I wore under my daring new dress. In romance novels, men always liked when the woman wore her "fuck me pumps" during sex. Well, if that turned him on, he could have that too. Tonight was all about him, though the thought of his eyes darkening when he laid eyes on the lingerie turned me on like nobody's business. I would reap some benefits too.

I grabbed my clutch from my bed before I started toward the office, taking the stairs carefully. I normally didn't wear heels quite this high. All I needed was to break my neck before he could even arrive!

A whistle made me look up from my feet to Ellie ,who stood at the bottom of the stairs. "Are you sure you're going out?" she asked. "Because I think Brandon's going to take one look at you, haul you back up those stairs, and keep you in bed until you walk funny." She giggled. "We won't see you for at least a week."

Charlie peeked out of her office as I reached the bottom. "I don't need to hear about sibling sex, thank you very much." She put her fingers in her ears with an exaggerated, "La, la, la!"

After Ellie tugged one of Charlie's hands away from her head, they followed me into my office where I started straightening papers. I didn't have anything else to do until

Brandon arrived. I may as well be somewhat useful while I waited. "Do either of you have plans for tonight?"

My sister shook her head. "No, just Freya and William and bedtime stories before I fall asleep at seven. You should remember how often I fell asleep on the sofa when I was pregnant with Freya." She brushed her hand over her tiny bump. She was only a little over three months along but Ellie's petite frame didn't do much to hide her pregnancy. She'd shown early with Freya, and this baby was no different.

When I looked at Charlie, she gave a one-shouldered shrug. "I'll probably go to the gym before I round out my exciting night with a rousing home improvement show and a gourmet protein shake. You know me. I live the high life."

The bell on the door echoed back to my office, and my heart skittered in my chest at the sound. He'd made it! I smoothed my hands down my hips. I couldn't wait to see his face. With a tiny squeal at the girls, I hurried around my desk and to the reception area, freezing in place. No fucking way!

"Hi, Jena."

"What are you doing here?" There was no way Connor missed the edge in my voice. I'd never used it with him before. He had to know I wasn't pleased to see him.

His eyes roved down my body exactly as they had that day in the grocery store, forcing me to suppress a shudder. We weren't dating. We weren't anything. That look made my flesh crawl. If I hadn't been anticipating Brandon arriving any moment, I would've gone straight upstairs and showered thoroughly, scrubbing my skin until it was all kinds of raw.

Connor spoke when his eyes finally found mine again. "I thought maybe we could get some coffee and talk." A heavy chuckle came from his chest while he scratched the back of his neck. "You look amazing. Maybe I should take you out for a glass of wine instead?"

My hands clenched at my sides. I stood so rigidly straight, a pole might as well have been strapped to my back. "Connor, I've already told you that I've moved on. If you recall, I insisted you do the same. I'm not going anywhere with you. In fact, I have plans tonight, and they don't include you."

He took a step forward, prompting me to take an equal step back. "I know I hurt you. I just want a chance to fix things between us."

An incredulous bark burst from my chest as my self-control splintered into dust. "There is no us. Until recently, you were with Lacy, and I'm currently with someone else. I'm not interested in having a cup of coffee with you, I'm not interested in sipping wine and shooting the shit about where we went wrong, and I'm sure as hell not interested in picking up where we left off." I propped my hands on my hips, gripping my waist. "I've realized a lot of things since we broke up, Connor. When we started dating, I may have thought I wanted you, but I know now that I yearned for something, no, someone, different. That probably sounds strange, but it's true. I never loved you, and I'm happier without you than I ever was when we were together."

He frowned as he took another step forward. "You don't mean that. I remember how hurt you were when we broke up. Besides, as you said, I'm also not with Lacy anymore. I couldn't be with her when I always compared her to you—I still want you."

I thrust one finger in the air. "Firstly, I never said I didn't care at all," I said firmly. "I simply wasn't in love with you. That said, whether you're in love with someone or not, having them treat you like you're worthless is devastating. In the event it skipped your notice, worthless is exactly how you treated me. By cheating, you made me feel as though I meant nothing. Whether you're still seeing Lacy or even why you ended the relationship is irrelevant because *I don't want to be with you.*" I punctuated the last by leaning forward.

"I swear I didn't mean to hurt you," he said with his hands out, palms up. "I don't know why—"

"Whether you meant to or not doesn't matter!" My fingers dug into my hips. Had he always been this obtuse? A part of me had to do something or that part of me that had snapped would strangle him. "The point is that I don't want to be with you, and no reason exists for us to hash all of this out—there's no point! We're over and have been for a long time. I don't know why you think you can show up and try this now, but I *want* you to leave me alone. Do you understand?"

I didn't wait for an answer. Instead, I swiveled around toward my office as the bell on the door rang behind me. I never saw who it was. A hand to my elbow swung me around and cold, hard lips pressed to mine as another hand held the back of my head. I didn't have to see who it was to know this was wrong—everything in me screamed and protested because it wasn't Brandon. My body didn't light up like a firecracker, the contents of my stomach rose into my throat, and frankly, his lips weren't at all like Brandon's soft full ones.

I bit down as hard as I could on the asshole's lip, pushed him back, and put all my strength behind a swing of my arm, punching something with a sickening crunch. "What the hell!" The exclamation came out nasally and pinched since Connor covered his nose and mouth with his hands. "What the fuck do you think you're doing?"

My feet scrambled to regain the balance I'd lost from the swing, but I still managed to hurl an arm out and point at him. "Don't you *ever* touch me again or so help me God, I'll have you arrested. Do you understand?"

"Jena." When I turned, Charlie and Ellie stood behind me, but it was Charlie's voice that said my name. "You better catch Brandon. He headed right back out of the door when he saw Connor put you in that lip lock."

No, no, no! I hurried around the sniveling weasel, who'd collapsed to the floor whining while still clutching his face, and through the door as Brandon backed out of the driveway. I couldn't run in those stupid heels, so I pulled the strap on the back and kicked them to the side, taking off barefoot.

"Brandon!" Before I could reach his car, he drove away without so much as a glance in my direction. I dropped my arm from where I'd waved it in a futile attempt to make him stop, hitting my leg and nearly making me collapse to the ground in pain. Shit! I brought up my hand and cradled it in my opposite elbow. All of a sudden, my wrist and hand throbbed mercilessly, bringing tears to my eyes.

As I walked back toward the house, a police car pulled to the curb with its lights flashing. Two men got out, and I about fainted when I recognized the driver. "Jensen?" Charlie was going to have a fit of epic proportions!

"Hi, Jena," he said, closing the door and adjusting his duty belt. "Is everything okay? We had a call to this address for an assault."

My eyebrows shot up involuntarily. "I didn't make the phone call, but Ellie or Charlie might've. If you could get Connor Willoughby to leave, I'd appreciate it. I've told him to go more than once, but he won't listen."

The two policemen led the way inside while I grabbed my shoes from the porch. When I returned inside, Connor was on his knees in the waiting room, holding his face. "You broke my nose!"

Jensen whirled around with his mouth agape. "You did this?"

"He forced me to kiss him," I said with a shrug. "He had a hand to the back of my head, so I bit him and swung. I still can't believe I didn't miss."

"It was a brilliant punch." When Jensen turned, Ellie lifted her favorite eyebrow. "Hi, Jensen. How've you been?"

He laughed while he hauled Connor up by his arm. "I've been good. I moved back into town a couple of weeks ago. I gotta say that I didn't think one of my first calls would be for y'all, that's for sure." He glanced at Connor's nose and chuckled. "I'm impressed, Jena. I never thought you'd break a guy's nose. Some things have certainly changed since I left. If Jena has become a bruiser, has Charlie suddenly become a demure and understated lady? Now, that I'd have to see!"

Jensen's partner took Connor's arm and led him a few steps away where he began speaking to him, writing down information in a small notepad. As I returned to the conversation, a movement behind Ellie drew my eye. Charlie ran down the stairs with a wad of paper towels, but suddenly slowed and stared like a deer in the headlights until one side of her lips curled into an unattractive snarl. "What the fuck are you doing here?"

"Hi, Charlie," said Jensen. His smile vanished in seconds. "How are you?"

"I was good until you showed up. Like I said, what are you doing here?"

Jensen peered down to his uniform and gestured in Connor's direction. "Answering a call." He pointed to the other police officer. "I should introduce you to my partner, Dean." After scratching the back of his head, he propped his hands on his holster. "I moved back last month and joined the force. It's a long story." His partner walked forward and whispered something near Jensen's ear. Jensen nodded and shifted his stance. "I'd love to continue to play catch up," he said, "but we need to know what exactly happened?"

Once Charlie handed Connor the towels for his nose, we told Jensen how Connor arrived and all that had followed while Charlie remained oddly quiet. I glanced back at her at one point, only to find her chewing her nails as though she were trying to get the last bits off of a corn cob. Her fingers were going to become painful if she didn't stop.

While scanning his notepad, Dean said, "He admits that you told him to leave. Also, that he'd kissed you without permission. You have two witnesses that he forced the matter. It's pretty cut and dried, so we'll need to take him into the station."

Connor sat in the waiting room with the cluster of towels over his nose. He looked so pathetic. I couldn't imagine him coming back and trying this again. "No—"

"Yes!" said Charlie. "He may not do it to you again, but what if he accosts some other woman? You can't let it go."

"I don't know. I don't want any more drama. I have to find Brandon and explain what happened." While it was imperative I talk to him, a part of me was angry with him too. He couldn't have stuck around long enough to see me break Connor's nose, for crying out loud? Did he have so little trust in me that he bolted like his pants were on fire? I remembered how much it hurt to be cheated on. I would never, ever do that to someone! He, of all people, should know that.

Dean pointed toward my arms. "You should have that hand examined first. It's turning a spectacular shade of red. Based on the number of times I've hurt my hands boxing, I'd say you've done a lot more than simply bruised it."

Jensen stepped closer. "Let me see."

As I held out my hand, Charlie stepped between us. "Back off."

"Charlie," I said, chiding. "He's only trying to help."

She touched my hand carefully as Ellie approached and watched. "Taking that prick to jail would help us. We don't need either of them for anything else." Her hand held my forearm while she cued me to turn my palm up. "Can you wiggle your fingers?" I could barely move a couple of them, and pain exploded through my bones when I tried. "Damn." She muttered the curse while she shook her head. "We need to go to the ER before you go anywhere."

I so didn't need this! I wanted to go after Brandon and knock some sense into that thick head of his—with my other hand of course!

"Jena?"

I shifted so I could see behind Charlie to Jensen. "Yes?"

"He claims he kissed you and nothing else, but I need to ask you if he touched you in a sexual way."

Charlie huffed. "He kissed her. That's sexual." Ellie placed her hand on Charlie's arm. Hah! Like that would calm her down!

"Connor grabbed my elbow to pull me around. Then, he held my head while he kissed me. That's it. Why?"

His partner cleared his throat while he wrote in his notepad. "Because touching you sexually increases the charge to second-degree assault. For what it's worth, I think he's taken the hint that you want him to go away, but in the meantime, he's stewing in your waiting room. I mean he's staying put because I ordered him to. It's assault, so we *have* to take him down to the station and let the prosecutor decide how he wants to handle it. Once you've fixed up your hand, we'd appreciate it if you came down to the station to file an official report."

"I need to call William and let him know," said Ellie, pulling her phone from the pocket of her sweater. "Mrs. Langton doesn't need to leave any time soon, but I don't want William to worry when I'm late." At least she and William had Mrs. Langton, a nanny of sorts, who came and cared for Freya while they worked.

"It's good to see you again, ladies." Jensen gave a dramatic bow while he chuckled. "I look forward to catching up with y'all. All of us were good friends once. I'll need to catch up with Taylor too." He turned as his partner approached with Connor, and they disappeared through the door.

"Good riddance to every one of them," said Charlie with a growl.

"Charlie, that's enough." Ellie hunted the first aid kit out of Maggie's desk, took out a disposable cold pack, and broke the bubble inside, placing it on my hand. "We need to take Jena to the ER."

I shook my head. "Screw the ER. Take me to Brandon's house. I *will* talk to him before I go anywhere."

Chapter 14

Over Ellie's objections, Charlie drove us to Brandon's house, which sat dark and void of life. Charlie turned off the car as I stared at the pitch-black windows. His SUV was noticeably absent. Had he returned home at all?

"We should go to the hospital," said Ellie from the backseat.

I shook my head while I tried to unzip my purse. "No, I'm going inside."

"He's not here," said Charlie as she held each side of my bag, giving me enough tension to open the zipper and pull out my keychain with one hand. I set the keys on my thigh and sorted them until I found the round-topped key for his house. Awkwardly, I hauled myself out of the car and headed for the door. I couldn't explain why, but I had to know for sure.

Nothing in the foyer or living room appeared different at a glance, yet that changed when I entered his bedroom. Several drawers were opened, their contents missing. I peered inside his closet, which was now bare. He hadn't had much left at the house. He'd obviously taken what remained.

Charlie strode in and shoved the drawers into the dresser. "Aren't all of his clothes at the house?"

"No, he had a few left. He's taken them. Do you know where he would go?"

"Maybe you should let him cool off. He'll come to you. You know he will."

My eyes burned and flooded with tears. "He shouldn't have run away. I told him I love him! I told him I never loved Connor! If he has so little faith in me, then maybe he doesn't deserve me." I slammed his closet door, rattling the walls. Unfortunately, it didn't make me feel any better.

"You don't mean that," said Ellie, standing in the doorway.

"Oh, yes, I do!" The first wet droplet hit my cheek, and I swiped it away quickly. "I told him! I also told him he needed to trust me, or our relationship would never work. He had so little faith in me that he took off—he took off! I could've dealt with him punching the lights out of Connor, but he didn't even do that!"

"You know he can't." Charlie grasped my upper arms. "He became a black belt in martial arts while he was in the Army. Remember? He can't use his training unless it's in self-defense or unless he's helping save someone from something major—even then you know how careful he has to be to restrain someone rather than cause injury. Otherwise, he could get into a great deal of trouble."

I did know, but it didn't mean I considered it a legitimate excuse. "What about your parents?"

Charlie took out her phone and began pressing the screen. A moment later, it quacked like a duck. She sighed. "Mom said she and Dad are reading. She hasn't seen Brandon this evening."

"The vet hospital?"

"I doubt it," said Charlie, "but we can try. I don't have a key, so if he's there and he won't answer the door, I can't do anything about it."

Nearly ten minutes later, we pulled into the parking lot. The office stood nearly as dark and desolate as Brandon's house, only the hall lights burning for security purposes.

Where on Earth could he be? Most of the places I could think of were from our childhoods. They didn't exist anymore. "What am I missing, Charlie? He has to be here somewhere."

She sighed and shook her head. "If he wanted space, he might have gone somewhere you wouldn't know. We can't simply keep driving around like this. I'm taking you to the ER. You have to have that hand examined. I know Brandon would make you if he were here, so he'll kill me if I don't."

"I doubt that," I said under my breath.

"I agree with Charlie." Ellie leaned forward between the seats. "Give him some time. Let him cool off and talk it out when you're both calmer. Nothing can be fixed if the two of you are geared up for a fight." She turned on the flashlight on her phone and aimed it at my hand. "You're swelling from the tips of your fingers to your forearm. You've broken at least one bone in there. It needs to be x-rayed."

Before I could argue, Charlie started the car and pulled onto the road, headed in the direction of Marysville General Hospital. I didn't want to go to the ER. I wanted to stomp my foot and insist we find Brandon instead. The problem was that my fingers, my wrist, and everything in between throbbed like nobody's business. Without anything better to do, I rested my forehead against the cool window and let the tears I'd been holding in start to flow.

When we arrived at the hospital, a few people were scattered around the waiting area. One woman held a crying baby bundled in a heavy blanket. In the opposite corner, an elderly man stared hopelessly out the windows.

Charlie and Ellie took seats in the waiting area while I checked in at the front desk. We then waited thirty minutes before a nurse called me back for triage, immediately swapping the cold pack Ellie had given me earlier for a new one.

"We'll need to get that x-rayed," the nurse rattled while she typed on the keyboard. "I'll go ahead and call down to radiology and put in the order. There's no reason we can't get that done while you wait. Keep in mind that I have no idea how backed up radiology is. As much as I'd like to say they'll get to you right away, they might have patients from upstairs before you."

"I understand." Tears leaked down my cheeks more than earlier.

The nurse tutted when she peered over at me from her computer. "I know it hurts, dear. I'll see if the doctor can put in an order for something to help with the pain. Depending on the break, it might help with the splinting."

"You won't cast it?" asked Ellie from near the door. She'd come in with me but insisted on keeping out of the nurse's way. Charlie, terrified they'd start shifting my bones, stayed in the waiting room.

"No, we have to let the swelling go down first. I'm fairly certain it's broken, but we do need to know what kind of break, which is why we'll x-ray it. Then the doctor will splint it, so she doesn't do further damage before it's put into a cast."

Once she'd finished on the computer, she stood. "If you'll go back to the waiting room, someone will call you when we have a room open. In the meantime, I'll check with the doctor about that pain medication."

"Thank you." I followed my sister back out to where Charlie sat playing a game on her phone while she waited.

"Well?"

I dropped into my chair and picked up a magazine. "Get comfortable. We're going to be here for a while."

She pursed her lips and returned to whatever she'd been doing while I stared at the magazine resting across my thighs. Why had I even opened it? It wasn't like I was truly reading it. My brain kept whirring and whirring, considering locations I could find Brandon.

I still couldn't believe Brandon had simply walked out. Did he have so little trust in my love for him that he thought I'd take Connor back? Did he believe I thought so little of myself? Even at my lowest point after Connor dumped me, I would've never taken that asshole back. I might have my quirks and insecurities, but I wasn't willing to be with someone just for the sake of being with them. No one deserved a relationship where the other person felt that way. Besides, I wanted more—I deserved more. Didn't everyone?

"Jena." I snapped out of my trance when someone shook my arm.

"Huh?" My eyes traveled from Charlie's hand to her face.

She pointed to a man in front of me dressed all in white. "Miss Barrett? I have orders to take you for an x-ray." He pushed a wheelchair closer.

"I don't need that. It's just my hand."

"Sorry," he said. "Hospital policy."

Ellie couldn't go with me because of the baby, and Charlie, as always, worried she'd pass out at something. She was such a coward!

Once we'd walked into the x-ray room, he stopped and locked the wheels on the chair. "Is there any chance you could be pregnant?"

"No." Thank the Lord! Right now, Brandon's lack of trust stung intensely. I'd never been able to imagine how Ellie felt when she discovered William was married, and then not long after, that she was pregnant. At this moment, I had more of an idea than I'd ever had. No, it wasn't the same. Ellie's situation proved more difficult, but this made me admire my sister's independence and determination all the more.

After taking shots of my hand from multiple angles, the orderly wheeled me back to sit with Charlie and Ellie. The nurse fetched us not ten minutes later and brought us back to an examination room. Charlie surprised me by tagging along. I thought she would stay glued to that waiting room seat for the duration.

The nurse and the doctor entered almost an hour after I was brought back. The nurse brought me a small cup of water and a pill while the doctor sat at a computer in one corner, plugging away at the keyboard.

"You shouldn't drive after taking that," he said, before he hit one more key. "I'm Dr. Evans. I'll be looking after you this evening." He swiveled on the stool and grinned. "I hear you've been prizefighting." A snort came from Charlie, whose phone had gone dead about a half hour ago. Ellie chuckled.

"Sort of." He was attempting to make things more comfortable. Not that it mattered. I wanted to go home.

"She broke his nose," said Charlie. "She should've broken his balls."

The doctor laughed and scooted his stool over, so he sat in front of me. My shoulders went rigid when he reached for my hand. "Relax. I won't poke around on it too much. You've done a great job of breaking it." He carefully turned it thumb down, trailing a finger where a brilliant bruise was beginning to form along the pinky side from the knuckle to the wrist. "You've fractured both the finger and the metacarpal here, one of the bones in your wrist is cracked, and your ring finger is broken."

"Holy shit!" When I looked back, Charlie's eyes bulged.

Ellie stepped over to the computer, which had an x-ray pulled up on the screen. Dr. Evans wheeled himself back over and pointed to each break on the picture. "Right now, we need to get the swelling down. I'll also put in a referral for an orthopedist. Luckily, nothing is displaced, but it'll probably be put into a cast by the end of the week. I've written a prescription for pain meds." He handed me the paper. You'll want that for tonight. With several breaks, it might be hard to sleep without it."

With the click of a button, the screen turned dark, and he stood. "The nurse will return to splint your hand in a moment."

"Thank you."

When the door swung shut behind him and the nurse trailed after him, Charlie returned to her phone and Ellie took the prescription from me, saying, "We'll have to stop by the 24-hour pharmacy on the way home."

The nurse returned some time later to put my hand in a black Velcro contraption, have me sign paperwork, and provide home care instructions before showing us back to the waiting room.

"That was three hours of my life I'll never get back," said Charlie.

"Let's go home." Ellie nearly swayed in her spot. "I'm beat."

Even with the pain medication, I was wide awake and wanted nothing more than to find Brandon. If I knew where he'd hidden, I would've taken a car myself, despite the doctor's warning about the medication.

After a stop at the all-night pharmacy, we went home. Charlie dropped Ellie at her door before pulling around and parking in front of the house. I didn't want to sleep in that bed all by myself. It would smell of him. I couldn't handle that right now.

I kicked off those ridiculous heels the moment the door shut behind me, I changed into pajamas, and grabbed my pillow so I could lie down on the sofa. The television helped keep my brain somewhat occupied. It didn't work wonders, but after my second dose of medicine, I managed to slowly fall asleep.

I growled and let my injured hand fall to my lap. I couldn't do a thing with this stupid splint!

It was only Monday morning, but with the brace from the ER, I couldn't write. I could type with my other hand, though. I'd just finished keying in a flower order one-handed, which took much longer than it should have.

"Maggie would help you'd if you let her." Ellie stood in the door, her hand on the small swell of her tummy. "You need to stop venting your frustration on us. Charlie and I meant it when we told you to take the week off, you know."

"I know, but what would I do? Sit upstairs and think about how furious I am at Brandon? It'd only make it worse."

"How much have you truly accomplished this morning? I don't think working has distracted you all that much, sweetheart. Why don't you go upstairs? Go for a run if anything else. That hand won't keep your feet from working."

I slumped back into my seat. "I ran yesterday morning before I took the pain meds. The impact jolted my hand and was painful. I had to stop before I hit a mile. Besides, I have an appointment this afternoon."

"I rescheduled the White-Bowman meeting until next week." She put her hands up, palms out. "Their wedding isn't for a year. It won't kill your timeline. You've been in a foul mood, and they're new clients. I didn't want you scaring them away."

I closed my eyes and took a deep breath while I clenched my good hand. Ellie was only trying to help. "I'm going for a walk." Rather than saying something I would regret, I walked straight through the front door and crossed the street, ambling through the park to the Riverwalk. I strolled down the familiar path, watching the ducks bob and glide through the smooth, placid water until I stood at the very spot where Brandon almost kissed me.

I remained rooted to that spot staring at the light reflecting off the water. Something about the low branches and the dried leaves rustling on the ground tugged at a memory tucked away in the back of my mind.

Brandon walked ahead of me through the woods, shifting the low hanging branches out of his way. Dried leaves and twigs crunched under our feet and the air had that musty smell that reminded me of when I was little—when Dad raked the yard while Ellie and I jumped into the huge piles of leaves he'd made.

We didn't talk while we made our way down the trail where the trees eventually cleared to reveal a huge lake stretched out before us. The water was already dark and the trees on the other side stood silhouetted against an array of colors from the setting sun. As Brandon turned and headed down a path, a small inlet lay not far ahead. I followed close behind him as he scampered down a dirt incline, then reached back and grabbed my hand. "Don't slip," he said.

By the time we reached the small sheltered cove, the sun still hung just above the tree line. How much would we be able to see once the sun completely disappeared? It's not like we had lights to guide us out of the woods. "How are we gonna find our way back?"

"You can see the lights of the cabin through the forest. Don't worry." A naughty grin stole across his face. "Are you still gonna do it?"

I lifted my chin. I wasn't chicken. "Yeah. Are you?"

He pulled his t-shirt over his head, leaving him in a pair of jeans and sneakers. "Fall hasn't cooled the water yet. It's still warm."

My insides shook and I bit my lip. "Turn around."

"Why?"

I gave a huff and crossed my arms over my chest. "Because I'm a girl, you dork."

"Well, duh! It's not like I didn't already know that, you know. Part of skinny dipping is seeing the other person naked. Besides, it's not like we're boyfriend and girlfriend or anything."

I swiveled around and began unbuttoning my shirt. "It still doesn't mean you get to see everything."

A zipper dropped behind me, and after some rustling of fabric, a splash heralded Brandon's entry into the lake. "Come on, Jen! The water's not cold at all."

I held my breath as I took off my jeans and threw them onto some grass with my top. Even at twelve, I still appeared more like a boy than a girl—I had nothing really to see. Not that I wanted Brandon to know that! My feet hurdled toward the water, so the darkness would cover me before he could make out so much as my bellybutton.

The water wasn't deep, and it lapped against my skin without creating a chill. I made my way out to the middle where Brandon stood waiting for me.

"Was it that bad?" He laughed as I came to stand face to face with him, reaching under the water and pinching his stomach. "Ow! You didn't have to do that."

"Well, you could've been more of a gentleman."

He put out his arms and ran them along the top of the water. "I didn't look. I wouldn't have looked. You know that." One of his hands found mine in the inky black water, and his fingers entwined with mine. "Look up, Jen."

Since we'd been standing there, the sun had finally dropped behind the horizon. When I lifted my eyes to the sky, millions of stars like I'd never seen before littered the darkness. "It's beautiful."

"I knew you'd love it." He was smiling. I didn't have to see his face to know. His voice told me.

I pivoted on my heel and strode back to the office, not stopping until I stood in the door of Charlie's office. "Do you remember that cabin where we stayed for Labor Day weekend?

We went once when I was twelve and again when I was fifteen."

"Oh!" She sat up straight, her eyes bright. "I remember that place. What made you think of it?"

"I don't know. I just did."

Charlie pulled out her phone and after a few moments, it quacked. "It's up at Lake Jocassee. That's a long drive, Jena. Are you sure he went there? It's only Monday morning. I don't think he'll stay away long. He might be back tonight, for all you know."

"Well, he hasn't come back yet, and it's the only place I can think of. Whether I'm certain or not, I have to try."

"Do you need me to drive?" She put her pen to the side of her desk calendar and started to stand.

"No, thank you," I said. "I can manage. I haven't taken the pain medicine today. It makes me tired."

She nodded and started touching the screen of her phone again. "I'll send you the address to the cabin. It belongs to a friend of my dad's. If Brandon's there, you won't need to contact them to get inside."

"Thank you."

"Call us along the way, so we know you're okay!" she called through the door as I headed up the stairs.

It took me less than ten minutes to change clothes and get on the road. I'd thrown a couple of apples and a protein bar into my purse, since I'd be driving through dinnertime. Fortunately, I'd walked everywhere since the last time I'd filled up my car. I wouldn't need gas for nearly four hundred miles.

While I didn't crawl down the interstate, time certainly crept by. Was I wasting a ton of time by driving all this way?

What if he wasn't there? I'd have to turn around and make the long drive home. I wouldn't get back to Marysville until eleven or even midnight, and my hand was already beginning to hurt from removing it from the sling and propping it on the steering wheel. It was more out of habit than anything else, since I couldn't do much with the few fingers not in the splint.

I finally pulled onto the dirt road to the lake house around six that evening and slowly made my way until the trees cleared and the log cabin stood at the back of the clearing, just as I remembered it. My heart gave a jolt and my body instantly began to tremble as I pulled around the side, revealing Brandon's SUV parked in the back.

After I turned off the engine, I walked around the cabin and checked inside. Brandon wasn't there, although he'd left the door unlocked. Once I'd called his name, I closed the door and stood on the porch, scanning the tree line. Could I find the lake without him? I adjusted the sling around my neck and set off, using only my memory as a guide. Before long, I could see the water through the trees.

The path wasn't as clear as it used to be, but I found the turn and followed it to the cove. As the cove became visible, so did a navy-blue plaid flannel shirt and Brandon's broad shoulders.

A twig crunched under my shoe, and his head whipped around. "Jena?"

Chapter 15

His high-pitched tone and wide eyes were proof that he never thought in a million years that I'd be creeping up behind him out here. "What are you doing here?"

I'd thought I'd calmed some since Friday night, but now that I'd found him, all of it came rushing back. As soon as the question left his mouth, my good hand clenched tightly at my side while I released a harsh laugh that nearly made me wince. "I wanted to know where you were—that you were okay— which was more than you did for me the other night. Did you stay and check to make sure I didn't need you? No, you disappeared off the face of the earth. You weren't worried about me at all, were you? You simply ran out the door without even knowing the first thing about what happened."

He faced me with a frown creasing his forehead. "What are you talking about? You were kissing him—kissing Connor. What else was I supposed to do?" Why did people say things evenly spaced like that? I wasn't an idiot. I didn't need it spelled out for me.

"Oh, I don't know." I shrugged, and when my arms dropped back down, pain shot through my hand from the sling bumping my stomach. "Perhaps stick around to see what happened next. Stay to ensure you weren't wrong." I pointed my finger at him, leaning into it. "I had no intention of going or doing anything with Connor Willoughby. He forced me to kiss him! If you'd taken the time to look, you'd have noticed that his hand held my face in place, making it difficult to pull away— even though I wanted to more than anything. However, you didn't even stay long enough to notice, did you? Because if you had, you'd have seen me break his frigging nose."

Brandon startled. "What?" His mouth remained slightly opened. Yes, he heard me correctly. He didn't have to act so shocked.

"Yes, I hit him. If you hadn't left town, you'd also know that this morning, the Marysville prosecutor decided to charge Connor with third-degree assault. He'll likely serve thirty days in the Marysville jail and will have to pay a fine. They toyed with the idea of making it second degree, but usually, that requires the grabbing of an intimate body part. Luckily, he didn't go that far."

I brushed back the few loose strands of hair the breeze had wafted into my face. "I just want to know what I did?"

"I don't understand." He climbed up the slope ,so we stood face to face.

My good hand found my hip. "It's simple, Brandon. What did I do that caused you to have so little faith in me? Over and over I told you that I love you. I told you that I've never felt for anyone what I feel for you. Did you think I'd throw that away for someone who treated me like toilet paper?"

He blew out a ragged breath. "I'm sorry, but I remember how torn up you were when Connor dumped you. Even on the Fourth of July, you had this depressed look on your face when you saw him."

I threw up my good arm this time and let it slap back down on my leg. "Who isn't upset when someone cheats on them? It's humiliating and demeaning—like you weren't good enough on your own. They had to have someone else to fulfill them." I had a weekend's worth of frustration and anger that itched to get off my chest. "I may have been hurt when he dumped me, but I have enough self-esteem not to want him back.

"Once he'd moved on, seeing him happy bugged me. I freely admit that. What bothered me, however, was that he was happy, and I hadn't found someone. Did you ever consider that? I can tell you one thing: even if Connor crawled back on his hands and knees, he could kiss my ass. I would never take him back."

"I'm sorry. I didn't think—"

"Fucking right you didn't," I said through the weight pressing on my sternum. "You ran. You left. I'm the one who managed to pry him away so I could hit him, and Charlie called the police. Then, Charlie and Ellie drove me around town looking for *you*, while the police took him to the station. Of course, you'd already left, hadn't you? While they took me to the ER for x-rays, *you* were feeling sorry for yourself. *You* were driving your miserable ass here." Yes, I'd interrupted him. Yes, I'd cussed more than once. One thing was certain, *I* sure as hell wasn't going to apologize.

"I'm sorry." He shoved his hands into his pockets and closed his eyes. "I didn't know."

My finger pointed directly at his chest while every muscle in my body remained as stiff as a board. He was sorry? Right at that moment, I was too livid to care. "Because you didn't trust me. You didn't wait around for a measly two minutes." My eyes began to burn, and I blinked, trying to keep the tears at bay.

I pivoted on my heel and rushed in the opposite direction. Tears ran down my cheeks in rivers, but I needed to get away. My feet kept moving while the dried leaves coating the forest floor crunched behind me. He was not only following but getting closer.

"Jena, please. I *am* sorry. I admit that I saw Connor kissing you, and I jumped to conclusions. I didn't know what to do, so I came here to think. I couldn't see you reunited with him. I couldn't face you only to have you tell me it was over. My imagination went wild. I admit it. Instead of confronting you, I wallowed in my own self-pity. Please! Can we talk? I do trust you. I swear."

"If you'd trusted me, you would have stayed," I called over my shoulder. I wasn't stopping, but neither was he.

"I have my bag packed. I was going to return tonight to talk—to convince you to stay with me—convince you Connor wasn't worthy of your time or your heart." Before I could emerge from the woods, he took my elbow and turned me around. "Jen, please."

My hand pressed to my chest. "I never needed convincing. Don't you understand? From that first moment that I gave you my heart, it was yours—maybe even before that. In the beginning, I may have second-guessed the attraction and Ellie's suspicions about both of us, but I let go of that fear and trusted you with all of me. You've always possessed most of my heart. It wasn't difficult to hand over what remained on a silver platter." I choked back a sob and shifted my hand to my stomach.

Brandon stepped forward and pulled me into his arms. His cologne and that smell that was only him flooded my senses, and my traitorous body nearly sagged into his, instinctually needing to burrow into him. It would be so easy to let go . . . I wrenched myself away. "No," I said with my palm out. "I need time to think. You have to give me time." His eyebrows pulled together in the center and his eyes shone in the light that filtered through the trees.

I couldn't do this anymore. Before he could stop me, I scrambled toward my car while Brandon rushed inside the cabin, emerging a moment later with a backpack and locking the door behind him. As I sat in my car, he threw his bag into his SUV and climbed inside.

Before I took off, I touched open my phone and pressed Charlie's number on speed dial. She'd wanted me to check in, and this way, I could talk while on the highway.

"Did you find him?" she asked right away.

"Yep, he was there. Do you remember the cove where we used to swim?"

"Yeah, I remember that place. My parents liked it because the water was so clear. You could see if an alligator was hiding under the surface."

I flinched but shook it off. It was funny how I never even considered alligators when we swam there as kids. Brandon and I snuck out on more than one occasion to swim at night too. "I hadn't realized that. Anyway, he was standing on the beach staring at the water."

"I hope you let him have it." Her voice dropped to that almost feral growl she used when she was angry.

"I did. He wanted to talk it out, but I'm still so upset with him. I'm currently on my way home, but he's following behind me. He claimed he was leaving this evening anyway."

Charlie blew into the phone. "Honestly, I'm glad he's there. I know you probably want space, but he's not the type to stalk. You're upset and he's upset. You'll both ensure the other makes it back to Marysville in one piece. Don't be stubborn and try to run him off. Let him help you. He *should* help you. You wouldn't have driven all that way if he hadn't been such a coward. Besides, he needed to know you love him, and that you don't want anything to do with Connor Dickface."

I sighed and wiped my cheek with the brace on my broken hand. "I just want to be home."

"You will be soon enough," said Charlie in a more soothing tone. "In the meantime, when you stop for gas, make him pump it."

A half-hearted laugh managed to force its way out. "I'll need to stop in an hour or so. Hybrids aren't great cars for distance travel, you know."

"Too bad you can't tie it to the back of Brandon's SUV and let him pull you."

"But then I'd have to ride with him."

"Nah! I'd stay in my own car if it were me."

Why didn't that surprise me? It's no wonder Charlie had yet to forgive Jensen. I wondered if she ever would, which was a shame. She still loved him. She wouldn't be so angry if she didn't. She'd also have dated since their break-up—something she never, ever did. Instead, she put all that time and energy into exercise.

"Drive safe, hon," she said. "Call me later if you need someone to talk to while you drive."

"Thanks." I sniffled just before the phone ended the call. A glance in the rearview mirror showed Brandon a few car lengths behind me. I sighed and continued until my gas light flickered on and I couldn't avoid stopping.

When I pulled into the next service station, I opened the outer door to my gas tank, but before I could get out of the car, Brandon was taking care of the pump. "I'm perfectly capable of doing that, you know."

He glanced up from what he was doing. "I know you are." He locked the nozzle to keep the fuel running and started to fill his own, returning to monitor mine since it had the smaller tank. "I'm certain this wouldn't be easy to do with that splint on your hand."

"Nothing is easy with this," I said, reaching inside my purse. "I'll go pay."

He shook his head. "I already put my card in the pump."

My body slumped. "You didn't have to do that."

"Why not?" he asked. "You wouldn't have made this drive if you weren't looking for me. Let me pay."

"Buying me gas and doing menial chores for me won't fix things. Besides, I chose to travel out here."

He put the nozzle back in the pump and shrugged. "No, taking care of you might not do me any favors, but I'd rather help you than leave you behind."

I ran inside for a coffee drink to give me a bit of energy for the rest of the drive home. Hopefully, the pain meds would counteract the caffeine by the time I went to bed and tried to sleep, not that I'd been sleeping well anyway. Maybe this time my brain would shut off the minute my head hit the pillow. Wouldn't that be a relief!

Brandon waited in his driver's seat until I returned and followed me back out to the highway. I don't know when I settled into the drive. I simply allowed my music to soothe me and lead me home. After I pulled into the driveway, Brandon's

SUV parked behind me, making me groan. I didn't want another confrontation. I needed to go to bed!

When I stepped out of the car, I shook my head. "Please go. I can't right now."

His hands shoved their way into his pockets. "I wanted to make sure you're okay. I'll need some of my clothes, but I don't have to get them tonight."

"Good." I swung the door closed behind me and dragged myself to the balcony stairs. "Call Charlie when you get home."

"Do I have to?"

I stopped half-way up the stairs and bent over the railing. "Are you afraid of your little sister?"

"Not usually, but after the set down you gave me, I am."

"Good," came Charlie's voice from the balcony. "Go home, Brandon. I'll take care of Jena. Maybe after some serious groveling, she'll let you back inside."

My foot hit the top step, and I leaned against the post. "I'm so tired."

She nodded and put her arm around my shoulders. "I know. Let's get you inside and into bed. You should be wearing the sling." The last wasn't the normal chiding Charlie usually gave but much gentler.

"I know, but I didn't want to drive with my arm in that thing. My hand might not be able to do much, but I feel more secure driving with it free."

She unlocked the door and turned off the alarm. "Then no more driving until the cast is off. Between the rest of us, we can get you around town when you need to be somewhere."

"Okay." I honestly had no intention of fighting at that moment. I plodded into my room, dropped onto the bed, and one at a time, removed my shoes. I'd worn a pair of leggings and a comfy shirt for the long drive. They'd work out just as well as pajamas, so I pulled the covers over me. A few moments later, Charlie held a glass of water in front of my face.

"Oh, my pills are in my purse."

She grabbed my bag from the floor and dug out the bottle. Once I'd taken the medicine, she took the glass and carefully elevated my hand on a pillow, setting a bag of peas over the top. "If you fall asleep, I'll take them off in twenty minutes and park my butt on the sofa. Just yell if you need me."

"You don't have to sleep on the sofa. I'll be fine."

"I know you will, but let me help you."

Charlie sat on the other side of the bed and turned on the TV. Once a re-run of some sit-com played softly, she relaxed back while my eyes began to flutter. Lord, I was so tired! The audience laughed on the show, and that was the last thing I heard.

Chapter 16

For the next few days, I ignored my cell phone. While I'd love to say I'd moved on with my life, dressed, and killed it at work during that time, I hadn't done anything useful since Monday—unless you counted wrapping myself in a blanket in front of the television something important. I did, however, venture out long enough on Tuesday morning to have a cast put on my hand. Otherwise, the pain medication made me drowsy, so at times, I slept. Other times, I stared at the screen while some brainless movie played in front of me. I couldn't remember half of what I'd watched. I'd completely tuned out the picture in front of me.

I shifted to take some of the pressure off my hip. How long had I been in that position? The quilt shifted and my nose wrinkled at the smell that came out of the depths. Ugh! How long had it been since I'd showered? My doctor's appointment was two days ago. I'd cleaned myself up before that, although I couldn't remember showering since. It was now Thursday. I had to have bathed at some point. Hadn't I?

Footsteps clicked up the stairs, but I didn't look to see who it was. Ellie or Charlie were constantly checking in to see if I needed anything—if I needed to talk, if I needed an ice pack, if I needed a freaking noodle bowl. It didn't matter what it was. They still asked. They treated me like a sick child home with a stomach flu instead of a heartsick adult, wallowing in her own misery. I grabbed the remote and began clicking through the channels, pretending whoever just walked up the stairs didn't exist. Maybe I should watch another movie? What DVD hadn't I played so far?

A rather sizeable vase of flowers appeared on the coffee table, making me frown. "Where did those come from?"

"Oh, look! There's a card. Maybe you should read it?" answered Charlie sarcastically.

As I pushed myself up from the sofa, she removed the small envelope from the midst of the pink and clean white mixed bouquet of roses and held it so I could pull the small card from inside. No poetry or flowery words graced the small white bit of stationary, only a simple message.

I miss you. Please talk to me.

"They'd be pretty on the table in the downstairs foyer," I said casually. I cleared that lump from my throat while I clenched my good hand, so it didn't shake.

"Jena, I know he behaved like an ass, but you're going to have to talk to him eventually. You're going to have to forgive him."

"I know I'll have to forgive him. I can be upset that he didn't trust me, though. That's not a small thing. How can we have a relationship if he doesn't trust me?"

A high-pitched disbelieving bark burst from Charlie. "You're kidding, right?"

"No, I need to decide how we go forward. Relationships cannot work without trust." My arms wrapped around me and hugged tight.

Charlie sighed and shook her head. "All couples hurt one another at some point. It's inevitable. You can't give up at the first sign of trouble. It's also not healthy to hold on to your hurt and anger and let it fester like an infection."

I shook my head. "You mean the way you've let go of yours and forgiven Jensen?"

"That's different and you know it," said Charlie with a hard edge to her voice. "We were also young and stupid. Something that neither you nor Brandon is."

With a huff, I tossed the card on the coffee table. "Lack of trust is not the same as him forgetting to put down the toilet seat or staying out too late with his friends. He assumed I would dump him for Connor."

With a sigh, she sat on the sliver of cushion I didn't occupy. "I know. He was a dumbass. Believe me. I've given him hell for it. He's also a pathetic mess right now."

"Good."

"You don't mean that. You usually forgive everyone and everything. Why can't you give Brandon the same consideration?"

I stood and dropped the blanket onto the sofa. "Because it's different." I stalked around her to my bedroom, wanting nothing more than to be alone to wallow in self-pity—not that I could do that forever. Obligations could only be delayed for so long. Eventually, I had to return to reality.

"Please bathe," called Charlie before I closed the door behind me. "You smell rank." As always, she was the epitome of kindness.

After I scanned my bedroom, my hand went to my forehead. What was I going to do? I caught a whiff of what came from my armpit and waved that hand in front of my nose instead. Charlie was right. I needed a shower. Maybe that time under the hot running water would give me some idea to get out of this house. It was beginning to feel like a prison.

Once I'd turned the tap, I let the water warm up, took off my smelly pajamas, wrapped the cast, and stepped into the falling stream as the first hints of steam emerged from the shower curtain. What could I do? What should I do?

I scrubbed myself twice over to ensure I'd removed all of the stink, washed my hair, and even shaved my legs. Who knows why I shaved those? It wasn't like anyone would be seeing them any time soon, although I suppose it did make me feel better. Regardless of whether anyone would see my calves, they were presentable.

Wrapped in a towel, I opened my laptop and bit my lip. I needed to get away. I had to think, consider what I should do, which was impossible where everything made me think of Brandon. We'd had sex in just about every room . . . no, we actually did have sex in every room of the upstairs. For a lark, we'd even tested out my desk downstairs late one night. I'd have been terrified to do that during the day. One of us would moan too loudly, then Charlie and Ellie would've never let me hear the end of it.

The problem was I had no idea where to go. I picked up my phone, scrolled through my contacts, and when I reached the name I was looking for, I paused and pressed it.

"Hi, sugar." The endearment brought a smile to my face, especially with Dad's long drawl as he called me his favorite pet name.

"I have a problem," I said with a sigh.

He chuckled through the line. "Well, yeah, but I daresay you'll get through it."

"I need to get away for a few days—"

"Jena, running away won't solve anything." His tone wasn't scolding, but I could hear the disapproval.

"I'm not running away," I said with a huff. "I can't think here. Charlie and Ellie are always around. Charlie's slept on my sofa every night this week. I don't need to be babied, but they do it anyway."

"Because they care."

"I know and I do appreciate it. I could use quiet, though. Some time to figure out what I want. Brandon sent me flowers today. They're beautiful, and Charlie thinks I should talk to him, forgive him. I just don't know if that's something I can do. I miss him but . . ."

"It hurts."

"Yeah."

He breathed into the phone. "Let me call you back. I have an idea."

"Okay," I said. "It's not like I'm going anywhere."

The line clicked, and I peered around the room. Now that I didn't smell like a gym locker, I should get dressed, pack a bag, maybe brush my teeth. My hand covered my mouth, and I blew into it and sniffed. Yes, I should brush my teeth.

As soon as I'd slipped my damp toothbrush into a traveling case, my phone rang. I didn't recognize the number, but just in case, I swiped my finger across the screen. "Hello?"

"Hi, honey. It's Melanie."

"Oh!" I thought I recognized the voice, but no one sounded quite the same on the phone as they did in person. "Is something wrong with Dad?"

"Oh, no! In fact, he's right here. He told me about your conversation. I simply insisted on calling you back because I have the perfect place."

"You do?" Yes, I was surprised. I'd gotten to know Melanie a bit more since we first met, but I hadn't expected her to have a solution for me.

"Tell you what. Get your bag packed, and I'll swing by in about thirty minutes. I'll take you out there myself."

"You don't have to do that," I said quickly. "I can drive."

"It's no problem. It's only an hour and a half, and with that cast on your hand, you shouldn't be driving anyways." I opened my mouth to protest, but she beat me to the punch. "I insist. Now, get ready. I'll be there in a little while."

"Melanie?"

"Yes?"

"I'll meet you on the corner of the park. I don't want Ellie or Charlie to know I'm leaving until I'm gone."

"Gotcha!" She didn't miss a beat. "Don't worry if you forget to pack anything. The house is walking distance to town."

"Thanks, Melanie."

"None of that. Now, let me go, or I'll never get there."

With a laugh, I nodded—not that she could see me. "Okay. See you soon."

I hung up and took stock of what I'd put into my weekender bag and my small rolling suitcase. Nothing seemed to be missing, so I zipped them up and slid my laptop into the middle of the weekender where it would be cushioned. I moved the contents of my usual purse to a mailbag style that I preferred when I traveled. The long strap made carrying it with the cast easier. I slung it across my body, which left my good hand free for my small suitcase. My weekender also had a built-in flap that attached it to the walking handle of my luggage, so I could take them together. I carried both from the room, so the rolling wouldn't attract the attention of those downstairs.

Pausing at the kitchen, I scribbled out a quick note that read:

I had to get away for a while. Dad knows where I am if there is an emergency. Don't worry!
Jena

I hauled my bags out of the French doors and down the stairs, not letting the wheels hit the pavement until I'd walked past Ellie's house and crossed the street. Yes, I was being a sneaky coward, but I didn't want to argue with them. They'd insist I was fine here, but I wasn't. The constant hovering and babying would make me crazy before long!

Thankfully, I didn't have to wait more than a minute or so until, true to her word, Melanie appeared in her classic Ford F-100. She helped me load my case into a wooden crate she kept in the back so her groceries wouldn't slide all over the tail bed, and we took the first road out of Marysville.

The drive was pleasant, and Melanie turned out to be good company for the ride. She chatted about anything and everything inconsequential, completely steering clear of my hand, Connor, and Brandon. Instead, we talked about my childhood and her own during the drive down. More than anything, she loved hearing stories of Dad and his antics when we were younger. I had some fun enlightening her on some of his better ideas—at least he thought they were his better ideas. However, that notion could've been argued.

An hour and a half later, we pulled up to an ornate iron security gate. Nothing of the property behind the fence could be made out through the thick trees lining the perimeter, but Melanie keyed a code into the box, opening the gate as if by magic.

"What is this place?" The one thing we hadn't discussed was where we were going. While we'd traveled, I'd seen one or two signs for Beaufort, so we had to be close to that town, even if we hadn't passed through it.

Melanie pulled into the drive and pointed ahead of us. "This is the house where I grew up. My parents left it to me and my brother when they died, but my brother didn't want his share, so I used part of my inheritance to buy out his portion. I've always thought I'd move back out here someday. Of course, life got in the way." She sighed with a slight curve of her lips. "In the meantime, I spend as much time out here as I can."

As the trees cleared, my jaw dropped heavily into my lap. Nestled between several huge oak trees dressed in Spanish Moss sat an enormous two-story historic wood house perched on blocks with a wraparound porch and shuttered windows. Several palm trees surrounded the house, but what made me gasp was what appeared to be a marshy riverfront running down the side of the property. It was amazing!

"You should see the sunsets," said Melanie with a smile. "It's a family place. You and your sister are family, so if you ever want to use it, just let me know—I'll be happy to give you the key. Just make sure you clean out the refrigerator and tidy up before you leave. Those are my only conditions."

I glanced over to her. She was simply letting me stay in this mansion? "It's amazing. Thank you so much."

With a laugh, she killed her engine. "Don't mention it. I love this place, and it sits empty far too often. Now, let's get your things inside, and I'll take you grocery shopping. Once you're settled, town is a fifteen-minute walk down the pathway over there." She pointed toward a trail along the water. "Since it's just you, you shouldn't need too much. I have shopping bags on the coat rack near the door. You can use those. They're more reliable than that plastic crap they use these days."

Melanie insisted on helping me with my suitcase. Once we'd deposited my luggage in the master suite, she showed me around the entire house. "I'm afraid there's no cable; however, you can find a ton of books scattered around on bookshelves all over the house," she said, gesturing to one of the massive bookcases, so laden the shelves slightly bowed, spanning a wall. "You're welcome to read whatever you like. I believe your father said you like to crochet?"

With a one-shouldered shrug, I shoved my good hand in my jeans pocket. "I haven't crocheted much lately, but I did bring a project with me."

"Well, if you run out of yarn or need more supplies, there's a craft store in town. I'll point that out when we drive in for groceries."

After she ensured I could work the antique gas stove and turn on the electricity if a breaker flipped, she drove me to the closest market, so I could pick up some food for the next few days. Then, Melanie and I cooked dinner together and ate at a small table on the porch overlooking the water. Once we'd cleaned up, she hugged me and drove off into the twilight.

The first thing I did when she rounded that corner was open one of the bottles of wine I'd purchased at the store; I'd decided not to take my pain medication, so I could have a glass or two. Even though I hadn't traveled half-way around the world, this was the closest thing to a vacation I'd had in years. Regardless of the reason behind it, I'd try to relax.

I poured myself a large glass and carried it to a rocking chair on the porch, sipping the rich, dry merlot while I watched the sun sink low against the water, almost like it would sizzle if you listened hard enough. In the meantime, the sky burst into an amazing array of oranges, purples, and reds right before the stars began to appear and the night turned pitch-black. I didn't move while I viewed the entire show—I simply sat and absorbed the sight before me.

Only the shadow of the crescent moon joined the stars in the darkness. I'd rarely seen such a spectacular sight as this in Marysville. Too much light from Charleston and the rest of the suburbs blocked a good bit of it out.

The crickets sang, the stars reflected off the water like tiny fairy lights, gentle waves lapped against the shore, and from somewhere in the trees, an owl called from the darkness. This was just what I needed. I could finally let my hair down without the constant checking in of Charlie and my sister. This was paradise.

A vibration in my sweater pocket made me jump, my body sagging as I pulled out my phone. I should've left the damned thing in Marysville! After all, this house had an old rotary model still connected to traditional phone service in case of emergency.

When I looked at my phone, I had several missed calls and a text.

I can't believe you left!

With my thumb, I slid the screen open and opened my text app. "I love y'all, but I needed space. Please don't be angry," I typed. The owl hooted once more from the trees and I clicked my phone to sleep, rose, locked the doors, and snuggled into the plush comforter in the master bedroom, my eyes drifting closed to the gentle sound of the waves outside my open window.

Chapter 17

My Converse-clad feet plodded along the dirt trail while my good hand swung at my side, the reusable shopping bags in my grasp. I hadn't bought too much when Melanie took me to the store, so by Monday night, I'd run out of milk, and I'd used the last of the bread that morning. I'd managed to avoid town so far, but I admitted to being curious about what I was missing.

The dirt trail ended at the start of a decked boardwalk with the water to one side and quaint touristy shops selling everything from fleeces to refrigerator magnets on the other. Melanie had said to walk to the main parking lot by the beach before I turned into town, so I strolled further down, enjoying the salt-tinged breeze blowing in from the water.

For probably the millionth time in the past few days, my heart squeezed as Brandon popped into my head. The simple truth was I missed him more than anything and anyone I'd ever known. Yes, his disappearance the night Connor showed up at the office hurt and angered me, but Charlie was right. I had to let all that go. In the back of my mind, that had been obvious; however, I'd had to have this time. My thoughts and feelings were a jumbled mess that required sorting before I talked to Brandon.

The simple gist of it was that Brandon never had a problem with trusting me—other than with Connor. Hopefully, what happened knocked some sense into that rock-hard head of his, and we wouldn't have another issue with trust again. I didn't want anyone else the way I wanted him. My heart, my body, and my mind all craved Brandon Taylor and like no one else.

The parking lot appeared. I made the turn a couple of steps later, but an odd sound made me stop and scan the area. What was that? I stood perfectly still and waited for it again. A moment later, a tiny mewl came from under a car, so I stepped from the curb and bent over to look behind the tire.

"What are you doing under there?" A small kitten clumsily moved around on the concrete. I couldn't just leave it there, so I swapped the empty shopping bags to hang on my injured arm and reached in to grab it. The tiny fuzzball squirmed when I picked it up, but I cuddled it to my chest where it calmed. "Are you all by yourself?"

I walked around the cars, but I didn't find any other kittens or a mama. I returned to the sidewalk, still scanning the area. As much as I hated to admit it, someone surely dumped the poor little thing. Right now, it huddled to my sweater slightly shivering while I steadied it with the fingers not encased in the cast on my other hand.

"Now, what do I do with you?" The itty-bitty calico mewed and closed its eyes. She looked so young, but man, oh man, was she furry. Dirty tufts of hair came out of her ears and her tail would be a bottle brush if she flared it. Why couldn't someone have done the decent thing rather than dumping her in a parking lot somewhere? If she had siblings, it's doubtful they'd have survived, given the way she looked at the moment.

I walked to the next street and was about to cross when I noticed a small pet store a few doors down the side road. Instead of heading on to the supermarket, my feet carried me to the small building that resembled an old-fashioned post office more than a shop.

The bell on the door rang when I stepped inside. I paused, expecting the squawking of birds or the hum of aquariums to fill the air, but it was quiet other than some softly playing music. "Hello?" I called. Enormous bags of dog food lay stacked against the far wall with chalkboard signs indicating price on the top, squeaky dog toys hung from hooks to one side, and shelves with crates and pet beds dwarfed the opposite wall. The middle space was filled with shelves of various products and what appeared to be pet-themed gifts.

"Did someone call?" An elderly man poked his head out of a door, his bushy eyebrows raised. "I'm sorry. My hearing isn't what it once was. I had to receive a delivery." As he stepped into the room, his eyes dropped to the small bundle in my hands. "Well, what've you got there?"

"She was up the road, huddled under a car in the parking lot. I know she'll need to go to the vet. In the meantime, I was hoping to get her some supplies."

When he approached, his hands gestured toward her. "May I?"

I nodded and helped pass the little thing into his palm. "She looks too young to be without her mother. I checked around the cars to see if I could find any other kittens, but I didn't see any."

He ran his fingers through her long hair and carefully peeked in her ears. "She'll need to see a vet. You're right that she's too young to be without her mama, though. I'll go take a gander in that parking lot after we get her settled to see if someone ditched any others. If you ask me, it's a crying shame when people are that heartless." He sighed and laid his large hand over her, helping to warm her while she huddled to his thin frame. "Unfortunately, with her state, if there were others, they either died from being left out for so long or someone ran them over without knowing they were there. I'm sorry."

God, I hoped not. "So, what do I do for her?" She was so tiny and helpless. I couldn't just dump her somewhere.

He eyed the cast on my arm and smiled. "Why don't I help you get her cleaned up and fed? Then, we'll get together what you'll need to take care of her. Will you be able to get home?"

"It's not a long walk but I also need to go to the grocery store. I sort of forgot when I saw your shop."

He ambled over behind the counter and pulled a bottle and a tiny comb from a drawer and another bottle from the back shelf. "I always have samples of everything. You'd be surprised how funny people can be about the smell of pet shampoo." He pulled a towel from under the counter and set it on top. "I don't like using flea products on a baby this tiny." With gentle fingers, he put some foam on the kitten and worked it into her fur. "This is waterless so it will be easy to use. Then, we'll flea comb her to rid her of anything using her as a food source. She really can't afford to give anything away."

A cloth bathed in vegetable oil was used to clean whatever bugs he caught in the flea comb before he took them into the bathroom and washed them down the drain. When he returned, he held a tiny bottle. "I fixed this while I was in the back." He pulled a chair from behind the register so I could sit. "Feed all of that to her. When she's finished, I'll show you what to do."

"Is there a better way of doing it?"

He showed me how to hold the bottle so she could eat and press my palm with her paws like she would her mother. While she gulped the canned kitten milk down, I looked up to the old man. "I'm sorry. I never asked your name," I said. "I'm Jena."

"Jack. My name's Jack." He nodded and ran his hand over the silver scruff that stood out against his dark skin. "Nice to meet ya, Jena."

"Thank you for helping with her. I've never had to take care of a kitten this young before."

"Once she's fed, you can leave her with me, so you can grab your groceries. By the time you return, my daughter should be here to take over. It's her store, now. I live upstairs and help out when I can. Anyways, I'll drive you home when she gets here."

"Oh, you don't have to do that. I'm sure I can manage."

He peered at me over the top of his black plastic-rimmed glasses. "Groceries, kitten supplies, and a kitten with your arm in that cast. I'd bet my eye-teeth you're supposed to have that in a sling too."

I scrunched up my nose. "I don't like the sling."

"No one ever does, darlin', but you still should use it." The words weren't bossy but came out in this grandfatherly way I couldn't be upset with. After she finished the bottle, he showed me how to use a warm, damp washcloth to stroke her, simulating her mother cleaning her. After, he put her on a heating pad in a box and covered her with a towel.

"Now, you go get your groceries. We'll be here when you get back."

"Are you sure?"

"I'm positive. You can use the bathroom in the stockroom to wash your hands before you go."

"Yes, sir," I said with a smile.

Cleaning up didn't take long, so fewer than ten minutes later, I strode briskly down the sidewalk until I reached the supermarket. I didn't need much, but milk, eggs, bread, chicken, and salad fixings were thrown into the cart before I grabbed some wine and headed toward the check-out, pausing in the pharmacy section. On an endcap was a display of heating pads. I threw one into the cart. Jack used one, and it might not be a bad idea with the nights getting cooler.

When I walked back into the pet shop, Jack's head shot up from a magazine he was reading. "That didn't take you long."

"I didn't need much. I bought a heating pad for her."

"That's good. She'll need the heat for a little while." He moved to the register and pulled out some supplies. "I have a bottle, a few cans of kitten milk, a flea comb, and that waterless shampoo, which is just in case you feel she needs it. Once she's stronger, she should clean herself. I also put in a trial of kitten food. It won't hurt to put a little in the box with her. They start eating some before they're weaned."

I paid for the supplies, and when Jack's daughter arrived, he helped me take the kitten and my bags to his truck. Once I was belted in and had the kitten in my lap, he frowned. "You never told me where you're stayin'."

"At the old Moultrie place."

Again, his eyebrows shot up on his forehead. "You don't say. Now, you look nothin' like Miss Melanie, and I know she had no children with her husband. Thank the Lord she left that good for nothin'. So, how do you know her?"

"She's dating my father. I wanted to get away for a short time, and she brought me out here."

"Sounds like Miss Melanie. She was always the sweetest thing. Happy too."

I smiled while I watched him talk. "I don't think she's changed much," I said.

Jack told me stories he remembered of Melanie while he drove me to the house. When we pulled up to the gate, he insisted I key in the code without him knowing. "I don't need knowin' any of that," he said adamantly.

Once he helped me bring everything inside, he waved while he pulled down the drive, leaving me and the kitten alone in that big, empty house. I looked down at the tiny kitten in the box. "It's just you and me for now." I sighed. "I said I was going to call Brandon this afternoon, and it looks like you showed up to make sure I don't chicken out. Let's go make that phone call, and afterward, I'll feed you some more. What do you think?" While I'd talked, she sat up and mewled louder than I thought she was capable. Looked like the food, warm bed, and sleep were just what she needed.

I sat in the rocker, set the box with the kitten in my lap, and pulled out my cell. I opened the phone and clicked on Brandon's name, shaking off the sudden case of jitters that came over me. I don't even think it rang before I heard a frantic, "Jena?"

"Hi," I said, suddenly tongue-tied.

"Are you okay? Charlie said you left town."

"I know Charlie and Ellie meant well, but I needed peace and quiet. They were driving me crazy with all the mothering.

I would've had to hit one of them over the head if they kept it up, and I didn't want another broken hand.

He exhaled into the phone like he silently laughed. "Okay. I get it. Did you find what you needed?"

"Sort of. I do want to talk to you. Do you think you could come here?" I scratched behind the kitten's ear and she began purring like she had a huge truck motor in her throat.

"Yes, whenever you want. I'll be there."

"I'm staying in an old plantation home not far from Beaufort."

"Let me talk to my dad. I'm done with surgeries for today, and so is he. As long as he's willing to cover me, I'll leave as soon as I can."

"Thanks," I said softly. "I'll text you directions. Whenever you can. I do need a favor from you, though."

"What's that?"

"Can you bring anything you would need to treat a stray kitten? I have kitten formula, a bottle, a flea comb, and some waterless shampoo. She's pretty tiny."

His warm chuckle made my heart skip through the line. "What've you done?"

"More like what've I cleaned up that someone else has done?"

"I'll bring a box of supplies. Is she dehydrated?"

"How am I supposed to know? I didn't go to vet school."

Another laugh filled my ear. "I'll handle it."

I gave him directions, but as I went to hang up, he squeezed in an "I love you."

After I set my phone on the table, I took the kitten inside and fed her. I'd need to get dinner going at some point. I was going to have company.

Two hours later, Brandon's SUV pulled in front of the house. The sun had only started to sink toward the horizon, so he could still see the house and its surroundings when he emerged from his car.

When I'd heard the sound of the engine and the tires crunching on the gravel drive, I'd walked around the porch to the front with the kitten cuddled to my chest.

"How did you end up here?" he asked, closing the door behind him.

"Melanie owns this place. She brought me out here and told me I could stay for as long as I want."

"It's amazing," he said, his eyes taking in every last detail of the front. He grinned and pointed to my new baby. "Is that my patient?"

"If you don't mind. Someone dumped her in the harbor parking lot either last night or early this morning. She was cold and hungry when I found her. Fortunately, I found a locally owned pet shop. The owner's father was amazing and helped me get her fed and set up until I could bring her to you." My throat developed a crazy lump, so I cleared it out. "I'd planned on calling you before. I swear I did."

"If you weren't going to call me, you would've taken her to another vet," he said seriously. "I know you, Jen. You wouldn't use someone that way." He grabbed a box from the passenger seat and strode up to the porch. "Where can I take a look at her?"

We took her into the kitchen and used the counter as an exam table while he checked her over. "She's pretty clean for a kitten you picked up on the street. Her ears have no signs of mites. She might have a slight eye infection; I have some drops to clear that up. If she was dehydrated when you found her, she's better now." He scratched the top of her head gently. "She's a cute little thing. Have you decided what you want to name her?"

"No clue," I said with a laugh. "It's not like I planned to pick up a kitten this morning."

Brandon glanced around the kitchen. "Something smells good. Did you make dinner?"

"It's nothing fancy. Just seasoned chicken breasts with salad and roasted potatoes." I set the kitten in her box. Not long before Brandon had arrived, Jack had brought a larger box to the house with a small temporary kitty litter pan. That way, she was set up with everything she needed when I couldn't watch her. I'd fed her just before Brandon arrived, so she curled up next to a small plush toy I'd found in a basket in the living room and fell asleep.

We ate by candlelight on the porch while the sun set. Afterward, we sat on a rattan love seat while we sipped our wine. I fed the kitten once more while Brandon washed dishes. He helped me move her box to my bedroom before I made sure the front gate was closed, and he retrieved his bag from his vehicle.

Rather than dirty more sheets to wash before we left, Brandon crawled into bed with me that evening. We started to talk about random things that had happened since Connor, but I couldn't remember how it ended. I suppose I fell asleep.

Chapter 18

A loud thump, thump, thump pulled me from my dream, my eyes opening to the room awash in morning light. My head rested on Brandon's chest, which explained the loud noise that woke me up. My leg was thrown over his hip. The night had been a blur. I woke once in the middle of the night to the kitten yowling. I fed her and put her back into her box, but she continued to yowl until I put her in bed with us. I jumped. Where'd she gone?"

Lips nuzzled and kissed my hair. "Good morning," said Brandon, his voice rough. He must have just woken up as well.

"I put the kitten in the bed last night. Do you know where she went?"

His chest shook under my chin as I looked up to his face. There, above his shoulder was the kitten, curled into a ball and sound asleep. "She was there when I opened my eyes."

"I had her next to me a few hours ago."

"Maybe when you rolled over and cuddled to me, she wanted to be involved." He wore a devastatingly handsome grin that made me want to rip those covers off and . . . well, I couldn't do that yet.

I pulled back to my pillow for a bit of space as well as clarity. "We need to talk about Connor."

"I know," he said softly. "I promise that if it'd been anyone else, I wouldn't have reacted the way I did. Do you remember when you moved into the garage apartment? Right about when you started dating him? I'd just gotten up the nerve to tell you how I felt. You were having that painting party. Do you remember?" I nodded. "I could tell when I walked up the driveway. You had this tilt to your head and this expression in your eyes I'd only seen after you'd been intimate with someone. I couldn't ruin whatever you had going, so I swallowed my confession back down and did what I always did."

"Pretended everything was perfect the way it was?"

"Exactly. The night the two of you broke up, you were inconsolable. I thought you loved him."

"As I said before, I thought I did too. But I didn't know what love was until you. Please don't be jealous or insecure about him ever again. I don't want him. I only want you. You have to believe me."

He nodded and claimed my hand. "I do. I know I'll have to prove that to you, but I will."

I leaned forward and brushed my lips against his, but a paw bumped my face. As I pulled away, the kitten yawned and pulled back the leg she'd stretched. "Wow, I save her, and she pushes me away from kissing you."

A laugh rumbled in his chest as the fur ball stood and crawled over him to get to me, a loud yowl coming from her as she did. "I'd say she's hungry again." He picked her up and kissed me with a loud smack. "I'll take care of her." As much as I wished he'd slept naked, he wore pajama pants as he bent to put the kitten into the box and carry her downstairs.

I didn't bother to change out of my white cotton nightgown, but my teeth had a much-needed brushing before I headed downstairs. While I opened a package of bacon, Brandon finished feeding the kitten and taking care of her. I had toast and a plate of the greasy goodness prepared and sitting on the counter when he put her back in her box.

"A woman after my own heart," he said with a goofy grin. "You know I adore bacon." As he took his first bite, a yowl filled the room. We turned just in time to see the kitten pull herself, so her head peeked over the rim of the box. Brandon picked her up, and she wiggled like crazy to get at his hand with the bacon, making him laugh. "No way. You don't need that much salt or grease."

I grabbed the sample of kitten food and put a small amount in a bowl. She didn't seem nearly so interested but tried to eat it when we put it in the box with her. "We could call her bacon."

"Bacon?" Brandon laughed. "If you wanted to go that route, you could call her Tuna."

I giggled. "Marlin?"

"Shark," he countered.

I took a bite and shrugged. "I think I prefer Bacon."

"You would." He picked me up and set me on the countertop. "What are we doing today?"

"Vegging," I said, as though it was normal.

"You? Vegging?"

"I know. It's a strange concept for me, but I've become rather accomplished at the art. We could walk to town, but I did that yesterday. Today, I'd rather read, walk around the house, or crochet. Maybe stare at your half-naked body."

He peeked down at his chest. "Why do I feel like a piece of bacon all of a sudden?"

"Does that bother you?"

That wicked grin I loved so much covered his face. "Not at all, darlin'. I'll be your piece of meat whenever you want."

"Ew. That sounds awful." We both laughed but finished our breakfast while we talked, kissed, and touched one another. I'm not sure why we didn't go straight back to bed, but we moved out to the porch after we ate. I read sitting lengthwise down the love seat while my legs lay across Brandon's lap, his fingers trailing across my calves, massaging my feet, and slowly making me simmer under that nightdress.

What he was up to was obvious, but I did my best to ignore it, even though I'd read the same darned page about five times. A light shower started to fall, which, as time passed, progressed into a downpour. However, Brandon never missed a beat. His fingers continued to tease up and down my leg, progressively going higher but never quite high enough.

Finally, I dropped the book to the floor with a thunk. "I give up."

He smiled as his fingers trailed over my knee and just under the hem of my gown and back down. My God, I was boiling alive, and it wasn't even that warm outside. All the caressing and teasing was too much, but instead of straddling Brandon and burying him inside me, I giggled while I ran out into the rain. The cool droplets hit my overheated flesh, relieving some of that pent-up heat.

"What are you doing?" he called from the porch. "You're going to ruin your cast."

"You're driving me crazy." I brushed my wet hair back from my face, tilting up to feel the cold water on my cheeks. When I looked back at Brandon, his eyes weren't on my face but his jaw was lax while he gawked at what was lower. When I glanced down, I could see why. My nightgown had gone virtually transparent in the water. He could see absolutely everything through the thin fabric. His eyes devoured the sight before him, and a prominent bulge formed in the front of his loose pajama pants.

I skimmed my hand down the center line of my body, but before I could say a word, he'd stepped down and in two quick strides was close enough to yank me into his arms, his mouth searing mine as he finally claimed my lips—truly claimed them. These weren't the careful, gentle pecks of the last twelve hours but an amazing, no holds barred devouring, complete with tongue.

My good hand clutched his hair while his fingers skimmed the remaining way up my thighs, taking my gown along with them. I wasn't wearing panties, so the cool air hit that spot between my legs and some incoherent sound burst from my throat. Two fingers plunged inside me, curling into that place that made me writhe while his mouth trailed down my throat and sucked my breast hard through the fabric.

Noises came from me with every exhale while his mouth continued lower. He hooked my leg over his shoulder and watched me with steady eyes as his mouth sunk between my legs. My knees almost gave out, but he held me with his free arm, my mind incapable of concentrating on anything but what he was doing to me. Despite the rain, every part of me burned while I struggled to keep from falling on my ass.

When I climaxed, tears leaked from my eyes as I cried out loud enough that surely everyone for three counties knew I came. I pressed Brandon to the grass, ripped his pants pulling them down, and took all of him, sinking down until he was fully encased inside me.

"Fuck, Jena." His eyes rolled back in his head, and I shifted forward while I rode him, my clit rubbing just so whenever I sank back down. His fingers wrapped around my hips, clutching me and bringing me back for every thrust. That familiar coiling began low in my stomach and started to spread, but before I could orgasm, Brandon sat up and wrapped his arms around my waist, plunging me down onto him fiercely. I couldn't move. I couldn't think. All I could do was hold myself to him while he took me higher and higher until I screamed as I shattered. My name burst from him just before his arms went lax, and we fell back into the wet grass.

When I could breathe again, I couldn't help but giggle. "Now, I understand what people mean by there's no sex like make-up sex."

"Jen, we need to get that cast out of this rain and dry it out."

"Kill-joy," I said as his chest shook.

When I could move my legs, I pulled myself off him, covering my mouth with my hand when I saw the damage to his pajama pants. He had to hold them over his hips as he stood. "At least they weren't something expensive—not that I care in the slightest. It was awesome how desperate you were to get me naked."

He grabbed my good hand and drew me back to the porch. After grabbing a towel from the downstairs bathroom, he dried the outside of my fiberglass cast and dabbed at the edges of the padding. "How much water got inside?" he asked.

"I don't know."

"I can't believe you ran out into the rain without covering it."

"It's not like it won't dry out." I helped him squeeze the edges.

He shook his head while he continued to work. "That's just it. The padding won't dry out. If it's too wet, we'll have to take you to the doctor to have it replaced, so you don't get a skin infection."

"Oh," I said before dissolving into giggles. "I didn't know. They said not to get it wet, but I thought it was more of a comfort thing."

An insistent yowl came from inside, so we hurried into the foyer where Bacon was trying to climb out of her box again. "She wants to be fed."

He cuddled the kitten to his chest. "I'll take care of it. Go get dressed and make sure your insurance card is in your purse. We'll need to find somewhere locally to get your cast replaced before it becomes too late, and we have to go to the emergency room."

Thirty minutes later, Bacon was fed, and we were changed into dry clothes. The operator for the insurance company gave me the name of a local orthopedist. Fortunately, his appointments were running early so he could squeeze me in before he closed for the evening.

I will admit that it was wonderful having the cast off for even a brief period of time. I could scratch my arm and see how much the bruising had subsided, which was not much at all. My doctor had forwarded over the x-rays, so Brandon was able to see exactly which bones were broken and the colorful black, purple, and blue splotches down the pinky side of my hand.

When we departed an hour later, I had a brand spanking new black cast, a plastic bag to protect it from the rain, and a friendly admonishment from the doctor to cover this one. I hadn't told him the truth on how it got wet; the old man might've had a heart attack if I had. I'd simply told him we'd been caught in the rain without my arm being covered.

Before we headed back, we stopped by the grocery store to pick up food to cook for dinner. Brandon carried the bags inside to the kitchen, but when I followed him in, my eyes fell to the box, and I halted in my tracks. "Bacon's gone."

Brandon set the bag on the counter and scanned the floor around his feet while I walked around the downstairs. "Bacon!" I'd just called for the third time when I heard that familiar yowl, and she came out from under a sofa in the living room. "There you are. Why did you go wandering off?"

While Brandon cooked, I held the kitten and sipped my wine. "I wonder if she's hungry again?"

"She's fairly close to six weeks. I think she was dehydrated and hungry when you found her. She's starting to catch up and not so starved anymore, so she's slowing down with the bottles. I'd wait until right before we go to bed. Then maybe she'll sleep through the night. By this point, she wouldn't be nursing nearly so much as she was when she was born."

"You make her sound like a baby," I said with a smile. In a way she was. One of her tiny feet stretched wide and relaxed, itty bitty claws extending and retracting.

"How long do you want to stay here?" He'd stopped chopping garlic, his eyes on me instead of the cutting board. "I haven't ever taken time off from the clinic, so when I told my dad I needed to go, he didn't mind, but I do need to let him know when to expect me back."

"What about your patients?"

"Mom's telling the owners I'm at home with some nasty bug or another. I don't want to leave him for too long, but I do love being here with you—just the two of us kind of hiding away from the world."

"Me too." I stroked Bacon's back with my finger. "Could we finish out the week? Maybe drive back on Saturday or Sunday? I'm not ready to go home yet either."

"Do you have a wedding to take care of?"

"No." I shook my head while I stood and put Bacon in her box. "I'll call Ellie and Charlie in the morning. Ellie already volunteered to cover my wedding this weekend because of my hand. The clients completely understood. My next obligation is in two weeks, and I only need to confirm everything is ready to go, which I can do Monday unless Charlie would prefer to handle that tomorrow."

"So, Sunday?" he asked while I took a sip of wine.

"Sunday is perfect."

He tossed the garlic in the pan with the onions and stirred while I stared at his strong arms and how the muscles in his shoulders shifted with every movement. Without thought, I found myself behind him. While my good hand snaked around his waist, my fingers skimmed the taut skin just above the top of his jeans.

"Jen, if you start touching me, the food will burn. Then, I'll throw you on the table and have you for dinner instead of the shrimp."

I grinned and bit my bottom lip. "I missed you and wanted to hold you. You can have me for dessert later."

His body tensed, and he took in a huge breath. "You know we bought that chocolate concoction you noticed in the bakery.

You're giving me all sorts of wicked thoughts about smearing that all over your body."

"But then I don't get any." Yes, I made my voice all breathy even though I shouldn't have been teasing him. Dinner wouldn't take long at all, and I *was* hungry. If he burned it, we'd be ordering something to be delivered. We'd only bought enough for tonight and breakfast in the morning. He shifted my hand to the prominent bulge in his pants. I smiled against his back.

"Do you feel what you're doing to me?" He said it in almost a groan while his fingers entwined with mine.

"I'll be good. I did only want to be close to you." I started to draw back, but he clenched my hand tighter and brought it back to his waist.

"Then stay."

I pressed a kiss between his shoulder blades. "I love you."

His shoulders relaxed, and he lifted my hand to kiss my fingers. "I love you too. I've loved you forever. It's always been us, and it will always be us. That won't ever change."

I shifted closer and held him tight, my heart full once again.

Chapter 19

"Jen!"

The tell-tale slam of the balcony door echoed through the upstairs, making Bacon's head pop up from where she'd been sleeping on my bed and a tiny trill rise from her throat. She stood and trotted toward the edge of the bed, pausing when she looked down.

"I'm in here!" I replied. The door opened, and the first thing that caught his eye was Bacon. A wide grin suffused his face as he stepped up to where she was perched.

"Hi, Bay," he said in the funniest baby voice ever. Before we'd left Melanie's, he'd shortened Bacon to Bay. She'd grown so much in the past two weeks, and so far, made it quite clear she was my cat. She loved Brandon, yet she followed me everywhere with the exception of work. She was still afraid of the stairs, so she didn't try to tackle those.

He cuddled the purring kitten to his chest and kissed her little head. "Did you have a nice day sleeping in our bed?"

"So, I've been replaced by my kitten. Glad to know your priorities, Taylor."

"Don't Taylor me." He gently placed Bacon back onto the quilt and swooped over to pull me into his arms. "You promised me a do-over tonight for my birthday. Remember?" He frowned as he peered down at my ratty old bathrobe. "I was looking forward to something black and sexy, and I come home to this."

"You smell like antiseptic and wet dog. Maybe when I want to bury my nose in your chest and take a nice long whiff, I'll put on something that will rock your world."

He gave me a huge smacking kiss and shed his long-sleeved Henley, followed by his jeans, shoving them into the hamper before all that glorious skin disappeared into the bathroom.

As tempting as it was to follow him, I'd been dressed for the past fifteen minutes while I waited for him to come home. I carefully unwrapped my hair from its towel and took a good look in the mirror to make sure I hadn't ruined the style. Though one or two strands had come loose, it hadn't fallen. I applied a bit of gloss and some mascara.

I'd given Ellie the dress from the night Connor ruined our plans. While Brandon would love that sexy bit of fabric, it was tainted somehow. I never wanted to look at it again, much less wear it. Instead, I'd gone and bought another little black dress with a deep slit up the front and spaghetti straps. That hot number was currently hidden under my robe. My black fuck-me pumps were still under the bed.

Brandon emerged from the shower in record time with one of my white towels slung low on his hips. He hurried to the dresser and put on a new pair of boxer briefs followed by his grey trousers and a snug black turtleneck that outlined the muscles in his chest perfectly.

While he put on his belt, he lifted his eyebrows at me. "Well? Why aren't you getting ready?"

I pulled my shoes from under the bed and put them on while he spritzed some cologne onto his shirt.

"Brandon," I said as sultrily as I could.

"Yeah." He turned as I stood and dropped the robe, which was followed promptly by his jaw going slack. "I've just been waiting on you."

He scratched the back of his neck while he gawked. "I . . . Maybe you should've waited until we were outside to do that. The only thing that would make matters more urgent was if you told me you weren't wearing any underwear."

"For that bit of information, my dear sir, you will have to wait until the end of the evening."

With a groan, he took a step toward me, but I held up my good hand, my finger pointing toward him. "No way. If you touch me, we'll never go out. I didn't get squeezed into this dress and heels to stay home. We're going, so I can feed you steak and dessert. Then we'll come home, and you can do whatever you like."

"Whatever?" His eyes held a dangerous glint.

"Yes, whatever."

He took me in from head to toe and back with a husky almost whimper. "This is like a present at Christmas only better. I'm dying."

I grabbed my clutch and Bacon as I sashayed by him. "Don't keep me waiting."

Bacon didn't like being shut in the storage room near the kitchen; however, she liked to climb up furniture. Unfortunately, she couldn't get back down, so we still shut her in with her litter box. I managed to close the door before she hurried back through as Brandon strode from the bedroom, shoving his wallet into his back pocket and picking up his cell phone from the bar.

"Let's go. You've made big promises. I can't wait."

"Are you okay?" I set my casted hand on the counter and the other on my hip.

"Not really. I'm going to have a semi all night, but be warned, I'm considering this extended foreplay. Just be prepared when we get home. You'll be lucky if we make it in the door."

"Before you do what?" I gave him a sidelong look.

That wicked lop-sided grin I loved appeared. "You'll just have to guess."

My skin prickled and parts of me gave a jolt. Lord, he knew how to get a rise out of me with only a glance and a few words. "Then maybe we should go." I struggled to get that out without letting on how he affected me. A part of me was ready to say "screw it," shuck the dress off, and let him have his way. I grabbed my wrap and made for the door before I gave in. "Let's go."

We drove to Riverside, opting for a candlelit table on the deck rather than inside with everyone else. The nights had cooled, but the restaurant had heaters to warm the customers who preferred the stars and the sound of the rambling river to the low jazz played through the indoor speakers.

Only two other couples were seated outside, and we all had opted for tables spaced away from each other. Brandon and I weren't the only ones hoping for a quiet romantic evening. Of course, Brandon was the perfect gentleman, pulling out my chair before seating himself. He opted not to share my wine, however, and chose his usual local craft beer instead.

"You look amazing." His eyes still wandered to the low neckline and my breasts while he took a draw of his beer. "You're always stunning, but when you wear a dress, it does something to me. It's like you put ice cream with a brownie."

"You're ridiculous," I said, laughing. I sipped my merlot and sank back into the cushioned seat. "Charlie and I had a talk today."

"Oh, yeah. That sounds serious. I hope she didn't butt her big nose into our business."

"No. She wants to move into the garage apartment. Micah moved in briefly when he broke up with his boyfriend, but it's sat empty since he moved into his new house." I tensed, not knowing how he would take the next bit. "She's commented in the past that she can hear things from downstairs."

He sat forward and cleared his throat. "What kinds of things?"

"Like bumping against the wall."

His hand covered his mouth as he broke into a barrage of coughs. I set my wine down and started to get up, but he waved me back. "I'm okay." It came out raspy, but he took a gulp of beer and swallowed hard. "Are you saying she can hear us?"

"She hasn't said, but she did once say that she heard Ellie and William when they lived in my bedroom. Anyway, I told her that it's up to her. Later on, Ellie mentioned something I can't get out of my head."

"What's that?"

"That we should incorporate that upstairs apartment back into the main house. We aren't looking for our own home, but it would make it somewhere we could live for a long time if we wanted. Adding that portion back would give us one more bathroom and two bedrooms upstairs along with the single bedroom and bathroom where I lived originally."

"I like the idea. I could contribute to the renovation. I have some money saved."

"I have money put away that I thought to use for it. William offered to draw up the plans for me and have his crew do the work, so it won't be as expensive as if we had to find a contractor." My new brother-in-law was being very generous. Of course, he also wanted to add solar shingles and a small turbine in the back and use the pictures and house as an example of what he could do with an existing structure. "He has a few other ideas, but that portion of the upgrades will be at his expense."

"Am I going to hate that part?" he asked with a chuckle and lifted eyebrows.

"No, he's just making the house greener. We'll probably never have to pay for electricity again. You've been living there as much as me lately, so I wanted to make sure you were on board."

"I like living with you. I don't want to live anywhere else." He picked at the label on his beer bottle before his eyes latched onto mine again. "I hardly have anything left at my house other than furniture I could probably donate."

I set my glass down before my shaking hand sloshed the wine over the rim. "I don't want you living anywhere else either. If you want, you can give your house back to your mom and dad and live with me."

He smiled, standing to step over and kiss me. "I hoped you'd say that." His lips pressed one more time to mine. "Excuse me; I have to make a quick trip to the restroom before the food comes. I'll be right back."

I followed his movements as he made his way inside . . . well, okay, my eyes never left his ass while he walked. It wasn't a bad thing that I loved to look at him. I'd never been so physically attracted to another human being before, and it still bowled me over sometimes.

"Hi, Jena."

The voice startled me back to reality, and I turned quickly to find out who had sneaked up while I was preoccupied with other things. I stiffened and gripped my glass harder than necessary. "I heard you'd been released."

Connor nodded and shoved his hands in his pockets. "Since it was a first offense, the judge gave me three weeks but the full fine."

"I know. Jensen, one of the officers who came that evening, is a friend from high school. "He kept me updated." I exhaled and shifted away from him, crossing my legs. "I hope you find what you're looking for. I'm expecting Brandon to return any minute. We're having dinner, and I'd appreciate it—"

"I'm not going to intrude on your evening. When I saw you from inside, I wanted to apologize to you both. Unfortunately, he left before I could walk around from the side door."

That explained why Brandon hadn't noticed Connor. Brandon entered the door closest to us while Connor exited through one on the other side of the deck.

"Anyway, I'm sorry. I don't know what came over me, but I should've listened to you. Since I was released from jail, I've started back at work and I've stayed in Charlotte—if you remember, I moved to a company in the city before we broke up. Anyway, my mother had insisted on having dinner close to her house or else I wouldn't have come out to Marysville."

"I don't expect you to miss seeing your mother. I hope you know that."

"No, I know you don't. The distance is more for me than anything else. I'm not sure why it bothered me so much when I saw you out with Brandon Taylor that night, but it did. It ate away at me until I lost my head. I'm seeing a counselor. I just wanted to let you know that I won't seek you out again."

Some movement behind Connor pulled my eyes away as Brandon took the last few steps toward the table. "Willoughby. I didn't know you'd be here." Brandon offered his hand which Connor shook hesitantly.

"I was just apologizing to Jena. I wanted to apologize to you as well." With his thumb, Connor pointed toward the glass windows as Brandon sat in his chair. "I should be getting back to my mother. Have a good evening."

As soon as Connor disappeared into the restaurant, Brandon stood and planted a long kiss to my lips. "How'd I do?"

"You were the perfect gentleman." I couldn't help but smile while I appraised him carefully. "How badly did you want to hit him?"

"With every fiber in my body. His nose appears fine while you're still in that cast. I wanted to break his nose all over again, so he'd be injured for as long as you are. Not to mention for thinking he had the right to touch you at all."

"My hero," I said, rolling my eyes.

Brandon dropped back into his chair and took a draw from his beer. "I wasn't jealous. In the event you were wondering."

"I didn't get that impression from you at all. You clenched your jaw while you shook his hand, which you usually do when you're holding back. You've done that for as long as I've known you." I drank from my wine while he gave me a heated look over the rim of his bottle.

"You think you know me so well."

"About as well as you know me."

He pursed his lips and narrowed his eyes. "That's pretty impressive then." He took a long draw from his beer and crossed his ankle over his knee.

I perked up and pulled myself taller in my chair. "Fine, tell me something I don't know about you."

That label on his beer bottle must've been extremely interesting since he began to pick at it again. He cleared his throat while he took a quick glance around us.

"Wow, it must be pretty bad if you're checking the tables around us even though we picked the most secluded spot on the patio."

He gave a convulsive shake to his head. "No, it's not bad, but it's embarrassing." He coughed and took another drink from his beer. "Before we started having sex, it'd been five years since I'd been with a woman."

Thank goodness, I'd put my wine on the table. "Five years," I said in a high tone.

"I told you that I started to fall in love with you while I was in the Army. Once I fell for you, it was like cheating to even go on a date with someone else. Guys I knew in vet school called me a 'monk.'"

"I knew it'd been a while, but I hadn't realized it'd been that long." One of the few things he didn't know about me lingered in the forefront of my mind, but the waitress showed with our food, and somehow the topic changed with the steak placed in front of Brandon.

The food never failed to be amazing at Riverfront, and the dessert made my toes curl in those ridiculously high heels. As we walked to the parking lot, Brandon's hand held my good one, our fingers laced and my head on his shoulder. Three glasses of wine had made me an exceedingly happy woman, not to mention a woman who wanted to get her boyfriend naked.

Buckled into the passenger seat, I couldn't do much to tease, but I toyed with the fingers of one of his hands, even sucking his index finger into my mouth.

"You're trying to kill me, aren't you?" My grin made it hard to continue for a moment. I wanted more than anything to make him feel as uncontrolled as I always did when he teased me.

When we arrived home, I stepped in front of him on the stairs, swaying my hips while I climbed up to the balcony. I pivoted on my heel when I reached the top and crooked my finger. "Are you coming?"

I opened the door behind me as he laughed and scooped me up, slamming the door behind him. My back hit the nearest wall before his hands pushed my skirt as high as it would go. His fingers met bare skin and he groaned into my neck. "If I'd known you weren't wearing panties, we'd have never made it home."

"Happy belated birthday," I said softly.

"Gah! My eyes!"

Brandon froze stiffer than a piece of molten metal dipped in water. "Charlie, you have five seconds to get out or my pants drop," he called.

"I needed some tea! Trust me, the last thing I wanted to see was sibling sex. Ew!" She rushed through the balcony door, shutting it and locking it behind her.

"Now, where were we?" He grazed his tongue along the line of my shoulder before biting my earlobe. "I have five years of celibacy I'm still making up for."

I couldn't stop myself from laughing—but I didn't laugh for long.

Two hours later, Brandon's arms held me tight with the back of my body flush to his. Bacon slept, purring on my pillow while we lay there in a heap of tangled sweaty limbs, my flesh over sensitized to anything that touched it.

"Tell me something about you I don't know," he whispered before brushing his lips against a particularly sensitive spot under my ear.

"I never really liked sex until you."

He pulled my shoulder so our eyes could meet. "You're serious? I mean, you told me that your first sucked, but that's not unusual."

I watched my fingers as they played with that patch of chest hair. "If you'd asked me before Ellie's wedding, I would've told you I liked to look at a nice male body, yet sex was just okay. I didn't need it. I satisfied myself more than my partners did."

"Ouch!" He winced as he rolled more on top of me.

"On some level, I knew none of them were right." I caught his gaze and held it, my stomach flipping and tumbling the entire time. "That night you kissed me on the beach, you took over control of my body in a way no one else had. From that moment on, I didn't want anyone but you. You've ruined me for anyone else."

"Good." He brushed my hair behind my ear. "Then we've ruined each other."

I smiled and pulled him down for a lingering kiss. "I guess we have—not that I'm complaining."

"That seems like a stupid thing to do," he said lazily.

We both laughed as we lost ourselves in each other once again. At least I didn't have to be at work too early the next morning!

Chapter 20

Dragging myself out of bed at eight on a Saturday was a chore, but I managed, chugging more than one cup of coffee while Bacon ate some canned food on the counter. When I left for the wedding an hour later, the little traitor had wormed her way into the crook of Brandon's neck where she happily purred like a freight train.

Nothing out of the ordinary happened during the ceremony or the reception, which was a relief. With the amount of sleep I'd had the night before, I doubt I had the brain power to deal with something too onerous.

I dragged myself through the door that afternoon to Brandon, standing in front of the stove in pajama pants that hung low on his hips. My bag unceremoniously found its way to the floor as I kicked off my shoes next to it and sidled onto a barstool.

"How was it?" he asked.

He set a plate of blueberry pancakes and the bottle of maple syrup in front of me and I melted. I hadn't eaten before I left—I never managed even a bite at the reception—and he'd cooked my favorite breakfast. Pancakes weren't exactly the best thing for my waistline, so I didn't eat them often. Nevertheless, at that moment, I could've eaten stacks of them.

"I love you."

He handed me a fork and I dug in, moaning when I put that first bite into my mouth. "You keep making noises like that, and I won't let you finish your food," he said with a grin.

I shook my head while I chewed and swallowed. "I'm too tired. I might just fall asleep on you."

"That wouldn't be much fun," he said, laughing as he walked around and started massaging my shoulders.

"Seriously, I might fall face first into my pancakes if you keep that up." I glanced around the kitchen, but there was no sign of the kitten. She usually stuck pretty close to one of us. "Where's Bacon?"

"Oh!" He strode back around the island and picked up a feather, brushing it next to a cracked open cabinet door. On the second sweep, Bacon's tiny paw shot out and started grabbing at the toy. "She found her way in there about ten minutes ago, and I haven't been able to get her out. There's an opening in the back where the pipes and electrical run behind the cabinets. She can fit but I can't get my arm through the crack to grab her."

I grinned while her paw patted around trying to hold on to the feather. "Once she comes out, we'll have to plug that hole and make sure the cabinets stay closed. I don't want her walking around in the pots and pans."

"She might open them on her own, you know. You didn't exactly find a passive kitten. She's probably more stubborn than my sister." The tea kettle whistled, and he poured some hot water into a cup before placing it in front of me. "Peppermint. I thought you might not need the caffeine after I cleaned out the coffee maker this morning. How much coffee did you drink?"

"I mainlined all morning. It didn't help much. I should've insisted on sleep much earlier last night."

He scoffed while he wiped the counter. "Cut me off? You can't resist me."

I knew that teasing smile well. "I think maybe you can't resist me." I pulled the next bite of pancakes off with my teeth while his nostrils flared just a little. "But I'd like a nap before we test our theory."

He laughed while we both turned to Bacon trotting out of the cabinet. He shut the door behind her as she rounded the corner into the storage room. "It's a pretty day," he said with a glance at the window. "Why don't we go out to the hammock? I have a journal article I need to read. You can snuggle up to me and take a nap if you want. Bay has been playing pretty hard for the last hour or so. She could come with us and sleep with you."

"That sounds wonderful. I just want to change into something more comfortable. This outfit will wrinkle like crazy."

"I wasn't going in my pajama pants. I'm still waiting on Charlie's inevitable lecture about last night."

I shook my head and sighed. "If she would keep up with her shopping instead of living at the gym, she'd never come down here except to cut through for work. I kind of doubt she'll even do that anymore."

When I'd polished off the last of my food, I changed into a comfortable pair of leggings and a thin oversized sweatshirt I loved because it was super soft on the inside and the wrist opening was big enough to fit the cast. I slipped on my Converse for the walk down, but since it was cooler today, I brought a pair of thick socks to wear in the hammock. At the last minute, I grabbed the book I was reading. It was doubtful I'd be awake long enough to read, but just in case.

Brandon looked crazy sexy when he slipped on a pair of well-worn jeans, a black t-shirt, and a plaid flannel shirt. "I'll grab Bay."

We piled into the hammock and Brandon covered us with an old quilt I kept for cool evenings outside with friends. Bacon found a perfect spot on Brandon's chest where she could also huddle against my shoulder. She purred and purred until her little motor faded as she fell asleep. It didn't take me long to follow.

My pillow was shaking, and my eyelid popped back against my eyeball. I groaned and pulled my head back. "What is that?" I opened my eyes to Bacon's outstretched paw and wide eyes.

"Your eyes were moving while you slept, and Bay thought she needed to investigate. She batted and bit at your eyelashes until she managed to pull your eyelid away and let go of it."

"You didn't have to let her," I said, my voice not at all the mature tone I usually used. Yes, it was a definite whine that would've made Freya proud.

"Darlin', it was too cute to stop."

"You two look comfy." Ellie rounded the tree pulling William behind her by the hand. "It's a great day for the hammock."

"They look more relaxed than they did last night," came Charlie's voice from further away. When I peered up, she was coming down the stairs. "Before you say anything, Brother dear, I won't be passing through the balcony anymore, *and* I'll call if I need to borrow anything. I swear. That's a sight I'd prefer to never lay eyes on again."

William and Ellie laughed. "What did she walk in on?" asked Ellie. William had sat in one of the chairs and drawn Ellie into his lap, stroking her small bump reverently while she relaxed into him.

"Nothing," I said, propping my elbow on the hammock and setting my chin in my good hand.

Charlie huffed. "Nothing? It was just the two of them coming home from a steamy night out and trying to rip each other's clothes off right when they walked through the door. I'd come down for a cup of tea. I had no idea I'd see *that*. Needless to say, I took my tea bag and ran upstairs. While I waited for the water to boil, I washed my eyes out."

Brandon's chest shook as he laughed. "You're the one who let yourself in."

"Didn't you notice the alarm was turned off?" Charlie dropped into one of the chairs and folded her arms across her chest.

"Not really," said Brandon with a devastating grin. "I had too much in my hands."

"Eww! No!" Charlie waved her hands in front of her while Ellie and William burst into gales of laughter.

"Well, I'm moving into the garage apartment next weekend. That way, we all get our privacy."

"Why do you need privacy?" asked Ellie with that one eyebrow arched.

"I have no life," said Charlie, "but I don't need to hear or see either of your personal lives."

William turned to us without a pause. "So, do you want to renovate the upstairs as we discussed? I wouldn't bring clients through the house. It's more important to show them how the system looks on the outside. I can use the empty utility closet outside the back mudroom for the wiring and battery system."

"William intends on replacing our roof too," said Ellie. "He wants more than one example to show how much it can save on electricity and how it looks. It will be great to have no electricity bill for the office. The worst is the air conditioning in the summer."

"The roof does appear worn out. If walls are being torn down and replaced upstairs, we can re-insulate up there and help a lot with saving energy, can't we?" Brandon's journal magazine lay at his side, forgotten. Bacon, meanwhile, had forgotten about my eyelashes and was attacking our feet under the quilt.

"Definitely," said William, nodding. "We'll work it out later. I just want to go ahead and pencil it into the schedule and start work on the plans. I'll need to get some measurements this week."

I sat up, being careful of my hand. "Where's Freya?"

"Grant, Addy, and Ben took her to the zoo." Ellie chuckled and shook her head. William's father always found fun ways to spend time with Freya. "Grant likes to give us days to ourselves and, since I didn't have a wedding today and Addy and Ben were in town, he asked if they could take her. We're enjoying the quiet now since that time off will disappear once the baby is born."

Ellie peeked over at Charlie and bit her lip for a second. "I know it's a month away, but I was hoping to talk about

Halloween. We're taking Freya trick or treating, of course, but we wanted to have a get together after. Just family and close friends."

"Sounds nice," I said. "Let me know what we can bring."

With a nod, Ellie tapped Charlie's leg with her foot. "I want to invite Jensen."

"What?" Charlie's tone had that edge we always tried to avoid. "Why?"

"Because we were all friends in high school. I know the two of you broke up, but it doesn't mean you have to hate him for the rest of your life."

"You don't know what happened, Ellie. He was an asshole—is an asshole."

"You were both young," I said. "It's also been what?—Thirteen years since the two of you broke up. You could be civil to the guy."

"Maybe I don't want to." She crossed her arms back over her chest with a huff.

"For an occasional night?" Ellie put her hands together as though she were praying. "Please? For me?"

"Fine," said Charlie in a low voice. "But if he brings a date, I might just have to castrate him."

"Don't look at me for help," said Brandon.

"Oh, please! How long did I help Dad in the clinic? I could castrate a bull if I wanted. Not that Jensen's balls are anything close to that."

William's forehead dropped onto Ellie's shoulder while he chuckled.

"And on that note," said Ellie, standing and brushing her sweater over her slight bulge. "We're headed to the beach for a walk. Enjoy the rest of your lazy evening."

Charlie grumbled as she stood, trying to pet Bacon while the kitten rolled on her back and started to attack Charlie's fingers.

"You don't have to hate him forever, you know?" I said carefully. I didn't want to get my head bitten off.

"But I do," she said softly. Her tone was almost brittle. "I'm going to the gym. Are you going to church in the morning?"

"Yes." I pulled Bacon off Charlie's hand and scratched behind her ears while she tried to roll over and bite my fingers. "We're going to lunch with my dad and Melanie, though. I think they want to have Thanksgiving at her childhood home for the entire family. At least, that's what Melanie hinted at on the phone."

"That sounds nice." Charlie cleared her throat and put up her hand to wave. "I'll see you tomorrow morning then."

"See you later," called Brandon as she walked away.

Charlie rounded the corner, and I laid back down at Brandon's side. "She's got to let go of some of that hurt."

"She's held on to it for so long it's festered. She hasn't put it behind her, she hasn't forgiven him, and she hasn't moved on. The problem will be finding someone who can break down that reinforced steel wall she's built around her heart. You know Jensen came into the clinic last week with his dog."

"He has a dog?"

"Yes, a Jack Russell Terrier named Daphne. From what Jensen's told me, he's had a rough time of it the past few years.

Charlie needs to cut him a break but it's not like I can say anything to her."

"No, she'd see that as your taking Jensen's side."

A leaf from the tree flitted and floated down on the breeze, landing on Brandon's head. I picked it up by the stem and twirled it in front of Bacon, her eyes almost crossing while she watched it. Brandon and I laughed as she lifted both paws and tried to decide what to do. After a long minute, she pounced, tried to grab the new toy with her front paws, and kicked it with her back feet when she fell over. Within a matter of a minute or so, the leaf was reduced to small pieces that the kitten jumped back from. I picked them from the quilt, and she caught a string on the quilt that she played with while we watched.

"Do you have a wedding next weekend?"

"No, Charlie covered most of this month's weddings while I hid from everyone."

"Do you think Melanie would let us use the house?" he asked. "We could chip in on the power bill. I could fix the steps on the backside of the porch. That time alone with you was amazing. I want to do it again—cook dinner together in that kitchen, eat under the stars, make love wherever we want."

"Why do I think having unfettered sex is the best part of that scenario for you?"

He ground his arousal on my leg. "Oh, I don't know. Maybe because you keep me like this nearly all of the time."

"Maybe we have sex too much." I bit my cheek waiting for it.

His body twitched while he gripped and released the back of my sweatshirt. "Darlin', the way I see it, we've been together since we were born. We're making up for lost time."

I pulled myself up so I could see his face. "So, you're saying we should've been like this since we were infants?" The thought was slightly disturbing, and my face surely reflected that.

"Lord, no. Maybe fifteen or so. I could wait for you to be old enough."

Rolling my eyes, I settled my chin on my hand while Bacon's eyes started to drift down to sleep one more time. "You had a very good time dating in high school. Somehow, I don't think you would mind going back and doing that over again. I remember your more daring escapades. You told me everything, if you recall?"

A lock of my hair had fallen over my shoulder and his eyes followed the strands as he brushed them through his fingers. "I was young and stupid. Once I realized you were the only woman for me, I felt as though no one could compare. Since our first night together, I've known no one else would suffice. The time since has only made my feelings grow. I know what forever looks like, what it feels like, how much that kind of love possesses your soul. This is so much better than dating those girls because they were hot or popular or because they'd let me get to second base. I'd give them up to have that time with you."

Such romantic words deserved a kiss, so I leaned up and planted one right on his lips, complete with a smidgeon of tongue for emphasis. "While a part of me would love to go back and discover you sooner, I think all of our struggles make us appreciate each other more. If I hadn't dated assholes, I might not have realized how amazing you are, and if you hadn't pined for me, maybe you would've taken me for granted."

His eyebrows dipped adorably while he frowned. "So, we were meant to be together now. You don't believe we would've worked out before?"

"Maybe. Maybe not. As you said, it's always been us. We didn't have to travel to some tropical island like Ellie and William to find each other. We were always together. Our relationship has simply evolved into something different and better."

"Loads better," he breathed.

I smiled and shrugged. He was right, but that breathy tone made my stomach go all wonky and parts of me stand at attention. "I won't argue with that."

"Good. Now, about you, me, and Bay alone at the Moultrie plantation. What do you think?"

"I believe anything with the two of you sounds perfect," I said. Who was I to argue?

I settled back down onto his chest with Bacon, listening to the steady cadence of his heart. His lips caressed my hairline as he spoke low near my ear. "That's certainly the way I see it."

I had Brandon, I had Bacon, and at that moment, I needed nothing else. The dreams I had of the future would come. At one time, I doubted I'd have the life I always wanted—an elegant white dress and a candlelit wedding, perhaps a baby or two. Now, I no longer had this crazy urge to rush into anything. Everything I'd ever wanted was out there waiting for me. I just needed to hold on tightly to Brandon and enjoy the ride.

The End

Acknowledgements

Two wedding planners down and one to go! Thanks a ton, to everyone who reads this series! I hope you fall in love with the characters as I have and look forward to the next installment with Charlie and Jensen. I'd play dumb, but I'm sure you have some idea by now.

For my family, I always give my love and appreciation for their unwavering support. My husband listens to all my frustrations. Poor guy! He helped me out a bunch with this by copyediting this series for me. I've tried to enlist him as a proofreader before, but the guy doesn't read romance. He finally caved and used his wicked grammar skills to help me, although he needs to learn to stop marking changes to more than commas and missing words a week before release! Huge thank you to Betty for offering her wicked editing/proofing skills for one last read through before publication!

My children have chipped in on one book or another with either proofreading (the less racy books of course!) and sometimes title help and giving my cover a look for any issues. It's amazing to me that they take pride in what I've accomplished. They are always a part of it because I couldn't do this without them!

Huge thanks to everyone from the online forums who have supported me in the past and now.

I've had a number of betas along the way, but Carol S. Bowes has stuck with me from the beginning, or nearly the beginning and was my wonderful editor for this go around. We have become amazing friends, and she is always a willing ear or eyes when I need an opinion on anything from a book, to a blurb, to a random blog post. I've learned so much from her.

A huge thanks to my friends both in the military community and outside of it. Friends are precious and a good friend is priceless. I thank my friends for every willing ear and every laugh that's gotten me through a rough day.

JAFF is a relatively small and tight-knit community, and I love that. The support of other authors in the genre is absolutely fantastic, as is the support and devotion of our fan base. I was definitely reminded of that after the publication of the first book in this series. Thank you to everyone who has purchased my books, left me wonderful messages, left an amazing review, and followed me after reading one of my stories. I wouldn't be able to have this much fun without your support and encouragement.

Pride and Prejudice's Elizabeth Bennet, she is always in need of practice!

Leslie's books include: *Rain and Retribution, A Matter of Chance, An Unwavering Trust, The Earl's Conquest, Particular Intentions, Particular Attachments, Unwrapping Mr. Darcy, It's Always Been You, It's Always Been Us,* and *It's Always Been You and Me.*

www.ingramcontent.com/pod-product-compliance
Lightning Source LLC
Chambersburg PA
CBHW072222170626
46813CB00003B/1061